Seaside Stories
a tale of disaffected youth
by
Jim Brown

Published by

writemarkweb.wordpress.com

To Margaret-Anne Shelley who loved me enough to change her
name to Maggie Broon.
David Cowell who has worked hard to motivate all around him.
Vonda, Stan and Ray, the main people in my life and part of
my extended family.

This is a work of fiction and any resemblance between the
characters and persons living or dead is purely coincidental.

Extracts have appeared in the Soft Secrets an international
magazine by Discovery publications in Europe, Britain and
America

www.softsecrets.nl

Front cover: demonstration in Folkestone 1969

Final page: the author and friends

First published in digital format in 2011

10 9 8 7 6 5 4 3

November 2019

writemark brings publishing into the modern era. Traditional publishers have, and always will be, responsible for bringing some of our greatest writers to the public's attention. They have and always will be constrained by commercial parameters such as print runs and the economy. Now, with the advent of epublishing, this is changing. The only element absent from epublishing is an extraneous affirmation that a work is worth publishing. Now that is also changing. By submitting your manuscript to writemark, our Readers will assess your work and either award you the writemark or provide editorial advice. The writemark logo is a graphic representation of a monkey knot. This was chosen as the organisation's emblem because: 1. It is used to throw lifelines to ships 2. Its name comes from the fact that a monkey, having secured a grasp on something, never lets go and 3. The American hobos used it as a fraternal symbol - it seemed appropriate somehow.

The Sentinel Publishing takes the edited and proof read manuscript and turns it into a paperback and e book.

Do visit our web site at writemarkweb.wordpress.com

PART 1

HIGH TIME IN THE SEASIDE TOWN

The Marlow was popular with the dedicated drinker and for me it was practically home. I worked there occasionally and drank there permanently. Big Ray the landlord, with his weight, swagger and battered face, rarely encountered problems. Stationed in a corner of the polished bar with one foot on a beer crate, he would light up a cigarette and hold court over a captured, hung-over clientele.

The jukebox was silent, the one-armed bandit flashing; the foolish were still to arrive. Sandy MacLean and Paddy Murphy were struggling over the simple crossword in the daily newspaper. They would spend the best part of the morning reading out the clues to the bar. It was dangerous to be too smart and know the answers. When I met them, they'd only started drinking in the Marlow after being barred from the favourite haunt of the local ex-squaddies 'The Dragoon.' A dive, where every half-wit crook and maniac soldier convened. "Here you go Sandy I've got one for you," I laughed holding, up a kiddies' magazine, "a picture of a tree, four letters begins with T. Time stood still, outside the traffic noise ceased, the gulls stopped screaming and the world began observing a two minutes silence for what was about to happen. Paddy started to shift in his seat and Sandy's face froze, his one eye pierced me like a laser light. "Ya wee bastard, that'll cost you a fucking drink," he roared. The bar sighed and the traffic started up again.

Sandy hadn't so much lost his eye as had it gouged out with a beer bottle during a row with Paddy his old army buddy, over an escapade with a Billy Boy down Bugis Street in Singapore. Bugis Street was a market during the day, but under cover of the night the transvestites came tottering out and the street lived up to its international reputation.

Sandy had started to re-tell the story of the night Paddy had pulled a bar girl and taken her up to his cheap hotel room only to discovered after some frantic groping that the girl was a guy. Paddy had boasted "Well I'd got that far, there was no point stopping."

Tables turned and beer was spilled, as Sandy and Paddy tumbled out into the street and fought in the dirt. The ruckus only calmed when Sandy was hit in the eye with a bottle. Sandy MacLean fled. The few still left huddling in the corner thought that was that, the fight was over. Paddy righted the tables and started back into his morning refreshment. Minutes later Sandy charged back in with an axe in his hand and his bulging eye hanging from its socket. Paddy Murphy stayed stock still as Sandy buried the axe into the table in front of him. "Do that again pal and your fucking dead." said Sandy; the blood dripping and splattering onto the floor. "Sorry mate," said Paddy "I'm sick of hearing that story. Do you want me to come with you to the casualty department?" "Would you?" asked Sandy.

They had served in many places with their Scottish regiment. Wherever they had been or whatever they had done, it had fucked them both up. Sandy was in his late thirties and built like a pit bull terrier. He was a Scottish borderline psychopath who was no longer as fit as he had been. The strong brew he drank morning, noon and night was taking its toll. His stomach was swollen and sat beneath his ribs like a medicine ball. His black hair was dishevelled and greasy. Although much quieter, Paddy Murphy was more violent than Sandy. He retained his military bearing, standing erect at the bar, he spoke rarely but his message was loud and clear – "Don't fuck with me.

After this fracas in the Dragoon, the two Scots decamped to the Marlow bar. The relationship between big Ray and the ex- squaddies was not complex. They were good to have around when some of the younger thugs got out of hand, few could stand up to a demented Sandy with or without his eye patch and Paddy was the sort of animal that needed a humane killer just to slow him down. If there was no drink up front, Paddy and Sandy became the problem. Their main source of income was removing safes from vulnerable properties. The contents of the safe in the Working Men's Club was one such safe. They drank there on Sunday mornings, before the Marlow was open. It gave them an opportunity to snoop about. Martha the cleaner, usually let them in. She had a fascination for Sandy. Some women love a bit of the warrior about a man. Martha let it slip, as she handed over a couple cans, that there had been some dodgy geezers in the Club the previous night. She whispered that the safe was full of money to pay a dealer who was arriving with the gear the next day.

Prior to closing time, not judged by the clock, but by the staggering drinkers, Sandy slipped into the toilets and waited. Under cover of the moonless night and channel mist, Paddy returned with a van and tools of the trade. Sandy opened the club door. Yale lock, no Chubb back up. This was going to be a dawdle he chuckled to himself. He peered out with his one eye and hustled in Paddy. Paddy knew about angles and levers and how to use a piano trolley. With a fulcrum and block and tackle, Paddy and Sandy hoisted up the safe and expertly slid it onto the trolley. They found it impossible to manoeuvre the safe out of the door of the treasurer's office. They had a can of super lager and a think. They figured that somehow somebody had gotten it in there so it must be able to be gotten out. It's the door, it must be somehow catching on the hinges. "That there door is gonna have ta go", they agreed. A minute later the door came off its splintered frame. The two men finished their beer and got stuck into the task. Their sweat dripped as they shifted and twisted the safe, precariously balanced on the piano trolley. Sandy sought out another couple of cans. Had to be the door frame they surmised. Once again, the crowbar went into operation. The fascia wood shattered under Sandy's fury, only to reveal a metal frame bolted to the solid wall. Still the safe wouldn't clear the door. After few more beers they gave up, they were beat. If only they had read the club's long and illustrious history, they would have known that the room was built around the cumbersome safe. Villainy had always been a popular pastime ever since the town was a tiny fishing village.

I had arranged to meet up with Harry. We had only known each other for a few months. He had arrived in the coastal town heading for distant shores, but like many he had stalled in his attempts to take the world by storm. The seaside town was once a desirable Victorian destination. A resort to promenade and show off one's finery. Then came the lower orders from London. The town adjusted to the clientele. Coloured lights, loud music, bingo stalls and packed pubs. The cliff top gardens and bandstand the only reminders of gentler holiday requirements. Harry was distracted from his voyage of discovery when Mary Knox had flashed into his life. She lived above me in Alley gardens and not long after meeting her, so did Harry. We became firm friends when Harry recognised the tee shirt that I was wearing. It was a present he had given to Mary on one of her many birthdays. He confronted me and demanded an explanation as to why I had her shirt on. I told him Mary had left it in the shared bathroom and I had claimed it. Not satisfied he marched back up to Mary's flat and the shouting began. Mary claimed I was a sneaky little bastard who was probably wearing her knickers as well. Then she threw him out. Harry walked down one flight of stairs to my flat and claimed a space on the front room floor. He said I owed him.

Late into the night we drank and smoked and planned the revolution that would replace the establishments and their lackeys with Harry, me and our lackeys. Harry was from the Birmingham area and had been brought up in a caravan, travelling about with his father from one building site to another. When asked about his childhood he always grew vague. "It was muddy." he remembered. He was bigger than I was, a swarthy character with dark hair and a chipped tooth smile. I was slight, pale skinned and red-headed. I liked Harry, he was political, stroppy and took little shit from anybody, He was thrown out of the Communist Party for being too extreme. He believed that Oliver Cromwell was on the right track. I was unsure of the burning of the monastery bit, but otherwise I agreed with his take on Capitalism.

The door opened. It was Harry. He was helping a pale shadow of a man into the pub, Mickey Love was a daytime drinker, rarely seen at night. A gentle soul, tall, rangy and pale as the moon. Big Ray held a glass to the optic, as Mickey limped towards his cure. He placed the whisky in front of Mickeys trembling frame. "Give us a hand mate" he whispered. "bit out of sorts today." Big Ray held the glass to Mickey's lips as gently as a mother offers milk to her baby. "What's she done this time?" Big Ray asked. Mickey pulled up his trouser leg to show the violent scald marks.

"You gotta tell her mate. This isn't right."

"I don't like to." Mickey shrugged " She means well."

Mickey had a benefactor, a lonely widow who cared for him, tucking him up in bed, making sure the hot water bottles stopped him getting cold in the night. The whisky began its work and his body relaxed, his eyes light up and he laughed. "There's no such thing as easy money." He reflected as he took his seat in the corner. Harry bought me a pint while we waited for the Machine man. The miser owed us money for a paint job we did on his rundown premises

Half an hour later he stumbled into the pub like a drunken sailor. His collection of fruit machine cash box keys rattled and jangled from a chain on his belt. His nails were long and his hands ingrained with the filth of counting money. He was in his fifties and balding, with a grey straggly, nicotine stained beard; a cigarette smouldering in his mouth most of the day. When he coughed he whistled. Legend had it that his difficulty in walking was the result of a bungled hit by a coastal gangster. The truth was he had contracted polio, struck in the genitals as a teenager. He walked unaided except for walls, tables and passing strangers. As the day progressed his trousers slipped slowly down around his skinny backside. He was bad tempered, drank too much and washed too little. He was banned from driving and always needed someone to chauffeur him around the pubs and clubs where he collected the cash from the gaming machines and jukeboxes. That duty had been the privilege of me and Harry. We didn't get paid much, but we skimmed plenty from the take and we were supplied with beer in every club and pub where his machines were sited. We were often more drunk than him.

"Any chance of getting some money mate?" I asked the Machine man who was ignoring us, as he relieved the Juke box, pool table and a couple of one armed bandits of their takings "Take it off our bill for the paint job."

"The job was crap and the paint was probably stolen." replied the Machine man.

"Come on mate." I pleaded "I haven't eaten properly for days."

"Money for drink though eh? You guys can always find money for drink." "Alright," he conceded "Get them a pie each Ray. I was told to never give the workers food or was it money, probably both. It's hunger and poverty that motivates poor people." Big Ray stuck two dry steak pies into the oven and turned it on. "Keep your eye on things for a minute will you Ricky" he asked. The minute big Ray went into the back room with the Machine man, there was an almighty swallow in the bar. "I'll get these," I said. I set up the drinks and went to pay for the round. I rang up one pint, put some money in the till and took twice as much out. The day was looking up. "Thank you Ricky," said Harry as I slopped a beer in front of him. "I'll have that with my lunchtime pie."

Big Ray took the cash boxes into the back room to count and share the contents with the Machine man. The two men sat opposite each other in the empty snug bar. The coins from the cash box were tipped into a heap on the table between them. Then began a game, a ritual that Big Ray thought unique to him, but one that the Machine man played with every landlord and manager in the area. They eyed each other like nervous fighters. The counting began. The Machine man could bag up the money at four times the speed of the average landlord. He had perfected a technique that would have shamed bank tellers the world over. With swift blurred movement of his hands the Machine man had the bags filling up and stacked at his left arm like a factory production line.

Big Ray was waiting. The Machine man knew he was waiting and as the last few coins were being counted, he gave him his opportunity. He took his eyes away from the table for a few seconds as he rummaged in the briefcase at his feet for a receipt book. Big Ray reached for a bag of coins and flipped it into his lap. The Machine man snapped his head back up and almost caught Big Ray, who looked away. In that second the Machine man had skimmed two bags of coins into his briefcase the sound muffled by a thick winter scarf. He opened the notebook he kept for each pub and counted the take and made the split. Big Ray was pleased, the Machine man feigned disappointment. He held his coin-stained hand to his ample forehead and checking the previous figures said to big Ray,

 "Where's all the money gone? The machines should be taking more than this." When he removed his hand there was an imprint of his palm staining his receding hairline like the Turin shroud. By the end of every day the machine man was the colour of a Welsh slate miner, such was the disappointment of the official take.

He looked at Big Ray and became serious. "What about the debt Ray?" You owe far too much. Others are on my back. I know that you intend to pay, but business isn't looking too good for you."

"They've raised the rents. The breweries want me out," said Big Ray .

"It's that simple."

Do you think you'll get a manager's job?" asked the Machine man showing concern.

"At my age and with my experience not a chance, I know every dodge in the book and more. No, I'm out. They'll get some little prick in as a brewery manager. It's called progress."

There was a hint of compassion for big Ray. The Machine man stole money from all his pub and club customers. They had all mutually robbed each other for years. People like big Ray were the fuel for his dishonest business. "Debts have to be paid. Why don't we get you robbed? I'll get somebody to snatch your night safe wallet. Just put in what you owe me and claim for what you want."

"The police are wise to that," said Ray.

They're not interested. Times change Ray. You put the money you owe in the night safe wallet I'll get a couple of the boys to relieve you of it. An easy nights work. You claim off the insurance company and I get the money back, all is sweetness and roses."

"The takes right down. I'll have to ring up twice the amount of drinks I normally serve on a weekend for the till receipts to show that kind of money.

That Saturday night Harry drove the Machine man around a few bars and backroom clubs. Sandy and Paddy had another engagement. Harry stayed sober as the Machine man became drunk and barely able to stand. It was time to find a bed for the night. Although the Machine man had his own squalid flat, he had perfected a practise of sleeping on floors belonging to young women who had kids and no permanent man. One of his favourite places was at Julie's. Julie was a beautiful young blonde-haired Scots woman in her mid-twenties, who lived alone with her daughter Shona. There was just one problem, Shona was Sandy MacLean's child. Sandy rarely appeared at the flat preferring to stay away from the ones that he loved so as not to hurt them. It was worthwhile for Julie to accommodate the Machine man; he always left a little money for the stay. Sometimes he would make a drunken lurch and try to kiss her, but at the mention of Sandy's name, he soon stopped. Harry took the Machine man back to Julie's flat. Julie offered Harry a coffee and busied herself in the kitchen while the Machine man counted out his money; sucking deeply on his cigarette, sighing and groaning as he drunkenly checked each bag and threw the money into his briefcase.

He obscured the contents of the bags and envelopes by scribbling completely unrelated numbers on the outside of each pack. When he sobered up he often forgot his own system.

Julie was too good for Sandy MacLean, Harry thought, as he watched her tidy up the

kitchenette. Why she had followed Sandy and his

psychopathic tendencies until she became pregnant, he couldn't work out. Nobody could. Julia checked on Shona and brought the coffee through. The Machine man lay back onto the couch leaving his drink untouched and slumped into a deep sleep. "I think he's just had an orgasm," Harry whispered. "you hear him counting the money. He gets off on it." "Well at least he gets off on something," she said. "how are you getting on at Ricky's?"

"It's temporary I hope." said Harry

He watched her move. Her jeans hugged her hips. As she bent to hand him a coffee, her jumper slipped up from her waist and revealed tiny silverfish scars on her tight, slim waist. Harry started to feel warm and comfortable, Julia was beginning to affect him in a dangerous way. The Machine man was gurgling on the sofa. Julie pulled a large cushion from the corner of the room and sat down next to Harry. "What happened to you and Mary?"

"She threw me out. I was just one of the many," Harry continued "She's with that asshole Jimmy Dawes some of the time and down the bar the rest." "Mary is her own person. She's had it tough."

"I bought her a tee-shirt for her birthday. Next thing, Ricky walks into the Marlow wearing it, alongside the biggest smile I've ever seen."

"Ricky's Ricky." she laughed. "he's even tried it on with me and that takes some guts."

"How about you and Sandy? I could never work out how you two were together." Said Harry.

"He wasn't always like he is now. Sandy was never the product of slums or a bad upbringing. He was wild when he was young, but it was an exciting wild. Not the bullying drunk who can clear a bar with a glance or a sudden mood swing. That trait took a spell in the military to develop. I fell for the spark in his eyes and a smile that had me quivering. I was only fourteen but I would have happily run away with him. He was older. He wanted to do something with his life. There was only the coal mining or farming and Sandy wanted none of those. Him and Paddy Murphy joined the army together and they've been joined at the hip ever since."

"Do you think.?" "No, they're not, it's not sexual. They've just learned that together they can be intimidating and fear is a handy weapon to be used. That's all. When Sandy first left to go into the army, he kissed me like a cousin on the forehead and agreed to meet me on his first leave. He saw me as a kid. His opinion changed when he returned a couple of years later. I'm sure I got pregnant just looking at him. It took me a while after I moved down here to realise he was damaged goods. By then I had Shona to look after. He has never ever harmed me or Shona. But he's afraid that one day he will. So he stays away. He used to appear without warning as if out of a troubled mist when he was weak and sick from the drink. I told Shona he was a knight fighting in a foreign land. I sometimes believed that he was. He would come home and stay until he was fit and his wounds had healed or he got a call from Paddy, then he would be away again. He rarely comes back now."

Harry was beginning to understand the temptation of forbidden fruits. This was the last thing he needed, this strong attraction drawing him towards Julie. She nuzzled closer to the chair he was sitting on. He put down his coffee and bent his head towards hers. She laughed quietly. "You better be sure you know what you're doing"

"Well he won't mind me stepping in then." "What?" she exclaimed "he would chop you into stew size pieces if he thought there was anything going on. Anybody with any sense steers well clear of me." "Well I won't tell him." Harry whispered giving Julie a kiss on the cheek.

The bars and pubs had turned their customers

out into the chilled night. Those still thirsty were hurrying club-ward, the already full, staggering home ward. The taxi drew up outside the high street bank. Big Ray put a cigarette into his dry mouth, opened the cab door and walked the short distance across the pavement to the bank's night safe, the battered leather wallet tucked loosely under his arm. "Won't be a second." he shouted to the driver to gain his attention. He opened the night safe with his keys and went to put the wallet into the chute. Two figures bustled past him. Then took off running towards the corner. "Fuck me," he shouted to the taxi driver "those bastards had my money away. I've been robbed." The cabbie checked every mirror to ensure he was in no danger then got out of the cab. The two men, collars turned up high and hats pulled down low, ran into the safety of an unlit street. Then marched into the darkness.

Big Ray lit up and savoured one of his much-loved cigarettes. He leaned against the end of the bar and remembered. "It had been a normal bank run," he explained. "five of them, on my mother's life, there were five of them, big bastards, broken noses, scars." Big Ray tried to remain calm as he puffed up his cigarette and the role he played.

"And you ran after them?" I asked. Big Ray didn't look fit enough to run the length of the bar.

"Too right I did," he continued."

"Did you catch them?"

"I should give these up." Ray said looking at his half-smoked cigarette. "God if I had been a year or two younger. I used to do a bit of boxing you know." The whole bar knew. "Over six hundred pounds, one of my best weekends for years."

"Six hundred pounds? There must have been a few in last night. The pub's been dead for weeks. You must have been banging the pints into that till" I said,

"Oh I was." said Big Ray.

Energic Engineering was a two-storey brick building with a ramshackle workshop at the back and a flat above. There was an office on the ground floor with a showroom window looking on to the street. It was screened from light and prying eyes by years of dirt. A large wooden gate opened onto an untidy yard. On one side there were half a dozen wooden garages crammed with old Chicago Bell fruit machines. These had been bought by the Machine man as a job lot from a London gaming house. They were illegal, they paid out larger jackpots than the government regulated gambling laws allowed. They were to join other machines in unlicensed drinking clubs along the coast; where unemployed youths and alcoholic men whiled away their time and other people's money. The fruit machines were missing one essential component that had long gone out of production. At the end of the yard, wooden stairs lead up to a workshop. It was in here that things could be machined from scratch. Stan, a man over seventy years old, worked all day on a lathe making the pieces that would soon have the one-armed bandits operational. Old Stan would spend hours getting the lathes set up just right, time meant nothing to him. Not much meant anything to him. His wife had gone. She hadn't died or anything, just gone. When he retired she realised that the only thing she liked about Stan, was his engineer's wage packet. He was the one of those skilled men, a dying breed who prided themselves on their work and ability. If he didn't have the right tool for the job, he made it. If it didn't exist, he invented it.

From the yard there was easy access to the flat above the office via a wall and a balcony that lead to the kitchen. I was determined to get the money that the Machine man owed us for painting the outside of the semi-derelict premises. I climbed onto the wall and swung myself over the balcony and slipped quietly down the stairs and let Harry in the front door. Boxes and carrier bags stuffed with papers and invoices lay around the cluttered office. The place was a fire hazard and a sordid reflection of the Machine man's mind. We looked around the room. "There's money in here somewhere." I said. "I know it. He hasn't been to the bank in days." On a cluttered desk there were plastic bags filled with a mixture of coins. I picked up a bag and put it in my pocket. On the floor a heap of dirty washing was piled in the corner. I walked up to it and kicked it. The top shirt fell away and a box full of stuffed envelopes and the night safe wallet were revealed. "Leave it somewhere obvious and no one will ever find it." I said, staring at a mound of envelopes stuffed with notes, "It must be burglars that spread myths like that." Said Harry

We both knew how the system worked. I counted out the money and Harry scanned the envelope. Soon we had sorted out those that were genuine and those that were the Machine man's little bonus. There was a very large bonus. At first we agreed to take only what we felt was our due. Harry was adamant about that. We counted out the cost of the materials and our time. "What about Big Ray's money? " I said.

On Sunday evening after the last of the customers had left the bar, Big Ray and his wife Jan were collecting the glasses and ashtrays. There was a loud hammering on the side door. "Bloody hell," complained Ray "what now?"

"Come on let's leave this and go up," said Jan "it's been a hell of a weekend. You can do nothing until tomorrow." A plastic bag came through the large letterbox and landed on the floor. Big Ray picked it up and felt it.

"Well it's not dog shit this time" he laughed.

Come the following weekend, Sandy MacLean and Paddy Murphy were remanded in custody pending further investigations. Big Ray and the taxi driver had failed to recognised them but other people on the street had. Few mourned their departure. Big Ray put in his insurance claim. Me and Harry had our unofficial payment for the paint job and continued with our frugal cadging so as not to attract attention. We continued to harangue the Machine man for money or goods in lieu of wages.

The Machine man was pissed off and Big Ray was puzzled. His money had been returned, but he wasn't about to own up to that. Now that there had been an arrest, he was assured that he would get his full claim for twice the amount of money that hadn't been stolen in the first place. The Machine man swore yet again to stop drinking. He couldn't for the life of himself remember where he had stashed his bonus. Somehow though he knew he had been out flanked. A few days later he was back in the Marlow. I was buying a beer and the Machine man was standing next to me. "Where did you get that ?" he asked pointing to the coin in my hand.

"I don't know," I said. "I must have got it in my change."

"It's quite rare, I haven't seen one like that for years, let me buy it off you." offered the excited Machine man. "I'll give you a pound for it."

After much negotiation we managed to acquire an old transit van from the Machine man as payment for the paint job. He registered it in my name because I had supplied the scribbled invoice from my mate the painter. Harry was allowed to fix it up for him and to use it when helping him install machines and pool tables. The Machine man was suspicious of me. Certain I'd been involved in the robbery. He told Harry as much, but he couldn't be sure, so I was allowed to continue helping him. There was still no wage of course but we ate and drank well and were dealing in cash. The van needed a few things doing to it, the body work patched and filled, the brakes stripped, fixed, bled and adjusted, the wheels and tyres changed and major bits like the engine replaced. Harry could do just about anything with motors, except make money out of them. He was a scrap yard replacement master and a genius with a welding rod. He worked furiously for weeks on the new project. I accompanied him, standing about offering encouragement and slipping off to the pub whenever possible. Harry seemed to have a love of puddles and leaking oil. He was always lying in water. No matter how many times he shifted the van out of one pool of water, by the next day it would be sitting in another. I became convinced that there must be a kind of phenomena; an unknown puddle theory yet to be discovered. Harry spent his days spitting out engine oil, brake fluid and diesel until finally the van was ready to start.

When Harry turned the engine over, the yard billowed with eye watering fumes belching out of the juddering engine like a burning desert oil well. Harry soon had the wreck on the road, taxed, tested and insured for both of us. We sent off the ownership papers and drove the almost classic transit van out of the yard and away for a run. He went to collect Julie and Shona. He was spending more time with them now that Sandy was out of the way. He wanted his world and Julie's to change and he was prepared to work hard and risk all for the future.

Mary Knox had soon forgotten Harry. She was slim and swarthy and had the look of a gypsy

about her. She had long black hair and a figure
that she would expose as much as the law and
Big Ray in the Marlow would allow. Mary was
born and bred in the town and had a variety of
lovers. She wore tight hot pants and long knee
length boots. She looked every bit as alluring as
any of models that adorn the minds of men.
She'd taken up with Jimmy Dawes as a bit on the
side after she had thrown Harry out for daring to
suggest she might have slept with me. She had
slept with me, still did on occasions, but it was
the audacity of the accusation. She'd known
Jimmy Daws since they were kids. He was
almost family and that's how they liked it down
the harbour. Jimmy hadn't dumped his own wife
just kept her for the week days. They were both
from the fishing families where three or four
surnames served several hundred of them.
Jimmy had always been there for her when Mary
was growing up with her three brothers and four
sisters. Mary was the fourth child and first girl.
This positioning in the family ensured she grew
up fast. It wasn't long before she didn't want her
attentive brothers sponging her down and
soaping her up in the Friday night bath. There
was something exciting but cruel about her. She
always had a drink and a bunch of men hanging
around. Big Ray was unsure if she was, or if she
was not, making money out of the passing trade.
Just the sight of something that might be
obtainable had the drinks flowing and the money
passing. "I don't know what you're giving them

tonight?" Big Ray said to her, stroking his bulbous nose with two fingers, "but keep doing it. This ones on me." "Cheers Ray." she giggled "but that was a double I asked for." She could see Jan seething in the background, praying to the god that all plain women pray to.

Jimmy called by after a day in the club He rang the bell. Mary leaned out the window of the top floor flat.

"Jimmy Dawes what do you want?" Jimmy looked up, she seemed naked. "Fancy a drink." he shouted. "I've brought a couple of cans."

"Jimmy Dawes, I don't like you." she laughed, throwing down the front door keys. When he reached the top of the stairs the flat door was open and a smell of paint wafted through onto the landing. Jimmy walked in his long hair flowing, his lunchtime beer making him feel good. He had a couple of cans stuffed deep into his reefer jacket. Mary was on top of a stepladders, painting the ceiling in her brassiere and a pair of skimpy knickers. "I'm not changing for you," she shouted above the music.

"You'll do me just fine the way you are" said Jimmy getting as romantic as he could. She finished the patch of ceiling that she was working on and accepted the drink that Jimmy offered.

"Are you going to give me a hand Jimmy Dawes?" she teased.

"Just as soon as you like," he said.

"You best get that gear off then, don't want you getting covered in emulsion now do we?" Within minutes Jimmy was up the ladder in his underpants and Mary was in the kitchen cleaning up. It was never love but there were weekends of passion. Jimmy had a bit of money, rarely his own, but that's what being successful was all about.

The year moved on, winter made way for spring and spring for early summer. The weather improved and at last it was warm enough to take to the streets. Harry had moved out of my flat. He had taken a carrier bag full of his possessions and moved in on a semi- permanent basis with Julie. I hadn't seen that much of him. I had taken up with Holly Berry a young beauty who was waiting to go to university. She seemed unusually keen on me. Her parents were local businesspeople, her father worked in London and her mother ran a florist's shop. She took me over to Paris for a weekend break and while we were there the French students had taken to the streets and manned the barricades. I would have supported them of course, if I understood what they were chanting. I had to content myself with the tourist sites and the florist's daughter.

Revolutions don't come around too often. The bar was packed. Big Ray hummed his favoured tune, 'I'm in the money', poured me a pint and pointed out the couple. ""Organisers." I think? They've already been interviewed by the local radio." I glanced over. Seated at a table was a young man and a dark-haired girl. "When did you get back." asked Big Ray.

"I'm just off the ferry."

"You with that florists' daughter?"

"Yes." I confessed, "but don't look at me like that, she's well over sixteen."

"I'm not. So how was Paris?"

 "Great, she paid for everything."

"You're a heartless bastard."I took my beer and pushed my way over to where the couple were sitting. "Someone told me that you're here to start the revolution." I said staring at the girl. She looked Mediterranean, dark eyes and glistening olive skin. The man was fresh faced, his tangled blonde hair flopped over his eyes. He wore an army combat jacket, blue jeans and Spanish boots; the uniform of the handsome left-wing activist. He laughed.

"Just a march mate, a show of solidarity. People are demonstrating all over. In Paris the students took to the barricades at the weekend. "

"I was there," I said.

"Were you ? I'm impressed, who were you with?" asked the girl.

"Less said the better. No names no pack drill."

"You'll be up for carrying a banner then." she said.

"I'm up for anything."

"Good," she said. "You can help me." I walked back to the bar and Big Ray filled up my glass. "I'm smitten Ray, dark eyes, swarthy skin. I think it's genetic, deep down I've always had a feeling that I'm originally from the Mediterranean.

"But you've got ginger hair."

"I know, I know."

"And your skin burns under a 60-watt light bulb."

"Gina Lollobrigita had red hair and she was from Italy." I said.

"Could have been dyed. I remember many a flame headed girl." recalled Big Ray, drifting back to a dangerous part of his mind.

Dogs barked and the police stood by. Placards were picked up, slogans were painted on sheets and colours were unfurled. The beer and wine flowed and the demonstrators were soon in the mood for revolution. The crowds surged and the chanting began. The swell of energy engulfed the marchers, moulding them into a unit. The crowd flooded the streets like a swollen river, the police crouched behind large plastic shields, their military helmets strapped down, their truncheons drawn. Something was in the air. Mounted police, snorting horses, sparking hoofs, riot- cops and students. Rastafarians with ringlet hair, union men and journalist, mothers with small children, the curious and the pissed. I held my side of the banner gripping the pole with all the fervour of the committed revolutionary and beamed at the dark-haired girl whose eyes held a world of promise. The credibility of the demonstration against the inequality of capitalism, was lost as the first shop window, a well known high street off licence, caved in under the pressure of the crowd. The police charged and laid into the marchers.

As in all conflicts there are no innocent victims, just victims. I was hit on the head and I keeled over in front of the dark-haired girl. She bent down to help me. I looked up into her eyes and pressed my head into her warm breasts, what better place to die I thought as I slipped into the warriors' abyss, a grave yard for heroes, I would be a martyr, they would build a monument to me in memory of my fight.

When I came too, I was lying on a single bed and the girl was getting dressed. "What happened?

"You were brilliant," she said.
"Was I?"

"A working-class hero. Got to rush." she said, struggling into her jeans and heading for the door. "Hand the key into reception when you leave."

"What's your name?" I asked.

"No names, no pack drill." she smiled, mimicking our first encounter.

Big Ray turned on the television in the almost empty bar. A Conservative politician explained to the news team that the responsibility for the country's slow decline over the last fifty years could be traced to the morals and drunken habits of the riffraff, ragamuffins and students who would neither work nor want. It was apparent from his Dickensian language that this member of the privileged classes didn't have his finger on the nation's pulse, but did have his head stuck well-up his wealthy arse. I couldn't believe what I was seeing. The images on the television showed library coverage of nervous young recruits attempting to repel an attacking mob. There were no images of the brutality of the police, no film of tourists and spectators fleeing from the heavily armed riot squad. Only haunting slow motion, almost arty shots, of an old Annie Knox, a local pensioner, once better known for her night time kindness to the sailors down the harbour. She looked terrified as she was approached by god only knows what, probably the police stopping her and her tribe of errant sons from liberating as much free booze as could be carried from the off license. Annie Knox fitted the image of frightened senior citizen as easily as the marchers were fitted up by the media.

"The world assumes that old people are always nice; that age is somehow a guarantee of goodness," said big Ray. "but in my experience, nasty young shits grow up to be nasty old shits."

The outside broadcast reportage returned to the television studio where the blonde student and the dark-haired girl were about to be interviewed. The girl adjusted the microphone pinned to her chest giving the camera crew an opportunity for a close up. "There's that girl." said Big Ray "she was a bit of alright.".

"Yep my head nestled among those beauties for most of the night."

"How is the head? Someone said you were the first to go down."

"I lead from the front Ray. None of this hiding behind rhetoric. Get stuck in."

"There's many a dead soldier had that philosophy." said Big Ray. On the screen, the blonde youth swept back his hair and began a well rehearsed tirade about inequality and injustice. "Doesn't sound very poor to me," said Big Ray. Didn't seem short of money either, stayed in the Royal last night and that's not cheap. One of those career revolutionaries if you ask me. Or an infiltrator, there's always plenty of them, he's probably a copper himself. She'll be his bit of stuff. She's alright though. I'd vote for her." said Big Ray.

"No she's not his bit of stuff;" I said. "the movement needs articulate people to speak for the cause."

"Bollocks," said Big Ray, "their hearts are on the left mate, but as soon as they get any money their wallets shift firmly to the right."

The bar-room door burst open. Jimmy Dawes entered with his bedraggled compliment of weary followers trailing in behind him. He began parading up and down, his long, matted hair whipped his drawn unshaven face. He ran the dingy working man's club, frequented by every would-be villain in the town. He was hyped up with his new found political awareness. He wore a military coat and swaggered like a kilted soldier as he marched and turned and posed and postured before his defeated troops. "When did he become political? asked Ray rhetorically.

"He probably thinks he can get a grant from the Workers Solidarity Party." I replied. "and if there are any going, he's probably already got it."

"Another pint? This ones on me," offered Big Ray "we had a good take yesterday, busiest day of the year. We should have a demo every week, brings out the best in folk.

A telephoned call warned Big Ray that the out of town policemen, who had been billeted overnight in the Army camp, were looking for a few beers before leaving the area. Big Ray agreed immediately to provide a free buffet and extended opening hours for the police officers and riot squad. He asked me to give a hand. What could I do? I was skint

 "Right lad," said a police sergeant, "any trouble from this lot and you come and see me and I'll sort it."

 I was almost comforted by the authority displayed. However, it wasn't long before the policemen, who were tired after their success at the demo, were pissed. The Police, having drunk the bar near dry and driven off every self-respecting punter in the neighbourhood, were turning on each other. Thinking it was time I invoked the Sergeant's instruction, I approached the police officer. "Scuse me Sarg," I said. "but the lads are……"

The Sergeant swung round and I looked into the eyes of a man who no longer knew who he was, where he was, or what the fuck he was doing there. It was apparent that the original plan was no longer viable.

Two bodies with flaying arms and legs, bounced about the floor behind the bar. A wrestling match that looked close to copulation. Above them stood Big Ray's wife who was shouting "You can't do that in here. Go to the toilets." Emphasising her Christian beliefs by hitting the excited policemen on the back of the head with an empty Babycham crate. Emerging from the pub cellar struggling with a carry out of drinks ordered by the Sergeant, whistling yet again his favourite tune 'I'm in the money,' Big Ray shouted above the noise to Jan. "Careful Pet, you don't want to hurt them. There're just lads having a night out." The crates of beer and the bottles of spirits were all safely loaded onto the riot squad van. Ray was about to receive payment when an out of town police squad car drew up. "Evening Landlord," said the grim faced driver. "I take it this was all paid for before closing time".

"Of course, officer" said Ray fighting back the tears.

Next day the town was returning to normal, I hadn't seen Harry for a while. He'd missed out on the demonstration. His revolutionary traits seemed to have lost their edge since taking up with Julie. I called across to see if anything was doing but Julie claimed not to have seen him since a major fall out a couple of days before and had assumed he was back at mine. I set off down to Marlow to look for him. He wasn't there. "Try the Club," said Big Ray "and when you find him bring him and the rest of the boys back here. They're spending too much time drinking in that dump.

The Working Men's Club was situated halfway down the High street Most of the workers had long gone to other affiliated establishments. The reason for going to a Working Men's Club was to talk about work with your fellow workers. In the club in the High Street few folks worked, even unofficially. Jimmy Dawes had been voted in by his father at the beginning of the year and seeing the possibilities had secured membership for all his pals from the seamier side of the seaside town. The beer was cheap. The licensing laws didn't apply to them. The police could enter, only if invited as guests. It was as if the sanctuary of the church had been adapted to suit the dedicated drinker.

Jimmy stood for election as the club chairman and treasurer. He was voted in. He stopped paying the brewers and everybody else. When the club was no longer credit worthy, the committee utilised their cross-channel contacts and stocked the bar with   illicit drink. Cigarettes were bought in bulk from the ferry crews whose first stop after their twelve-hour shifts was the club. The crews could have been described as workers that dabbled in smuggling but it was truer to say that they were smugglers that dabbled in work. In his own way Jimmy Dawes was a global thinker, a believer in free trade. The freer the better.

I looked out for stray police, skirted the High Street and came to the club the back way. There was no sign of any trouble. I banged on the metal door. a blind shifted and a familiar face peered out. He scanned the street in both directions; then clumped down the stairs to open the thick, reinforced door fitted after the attempted robbery. Ronnie Page leaned on his crutches and let me in. "Haven't seen you for a while" he said out of the corner of his wired-up mouth. "where have you been?" I helped Ronnie back up the stairs. Ronnie's left jaw had been broken. His left arm was in a sling and his left leg was in plaster. I was puzzled. The last time I'd seen Ronnie he was in hospital. A couple of Dutch dope dealers he had ripped off, had systematically broken his bones all down one side, but I could have sworn it was the right-hand side. "It was." said Ronnie. When I enquired.

"So, what happened?"

"I done it again, didn't I?" said Ronnie with a shrug.

Harry was slumped next to Mary Knox. She was stroking his hair and looking defiantly towards Jimmy Dawes. Mary Knox was a dangerous woman, she wanted nothing more than to see Jimmy jealous and brutal, beating Harry senseless. Harry had not appeared to miss her as much as she thought he should. "Fuck off Mary," I said smiling, as if I was wishing her a good day "go find a punter."

"Those that are not with us are against us." preached Jimmy twisting centuries of logic and scholarly rhetoric to suit his more personal motives. Harry sat up and broke free from Mary. "When did this new Jimmy appear? I asked "this is twice I've seen him pretending to be political."

"Since he's applied for a donation from the Europe Solidarity movement." laughed Mary. "He thinks he represents the working people."

"Come on Harry," I said. "time to shape up."

It was funny looking at Harry, he was normally the strong one. He'd taken something, downers or maybe he was still pissed. He was dribbling and muttering incoherently about Julie and life and changing for the better. I was beginning to wonder if we were really revolutionaries or just a work-shy member of the working class. Before he was put away, Sandy would roar with laughter when I claimed the police and soldiers would put down their weapons and embrace the rioting workers. "None of you lot have got a job," he would point out. "To the police and the soldiers your just unemployable scumbags." Well maybe Sandy didn't always know where he was or what he was, but he always knew what he was up against.

I met Holly after the lunchtime session and we walked down to what was left of the fair ground. I could feel the fire between us had dampened. The show was over. She was going off to University, a new life. The last thing she wanted was a summer fling with a waster to hold her back. A hard-eyed woman with nicotine hair screamed above the Waltzers. "Try your luck boy. Three balls for a shilling." I should have felt happier, she was here today and all night. I told myself to cheer up. Christ when I first met Holly I was as happy as a dog with two dicks. Even if it was just quickie behind the House of Horrors. I looked up and smiled. No. I wasn't about to miss out on one last night. She grabbed my hand and we started running, a leather jacketed youth and bright skirted girl, teasing each other into the exciting danger of a dark secluded corner. The sounds of Rocking Goose and Runaway filled the air. The diesel smell as strong as the pounding of my heartbeat.

I saw Holly off on the train to London on a windy Sunday morning. "No tears. No regret." She said. "It's the wind" I lied. I headed down to the harbour. On a Sunday lunchtime, the bars along the seafront competed to offer the best free bar snacks. Cheese and pickled onions, crackers, crisps and peanuts. A man could feed himself for the day by doing a pub crawl along the front. The easterly blowing in, roused empty bottles and sent cans clattering into doorways, rolling and tumbling, bouncing down the slipway, sailing off to sea. The harbour boats shifted on their mooring, rattling at their chains. The rigging, singing in the bitter wind, the tide drumming against the hollow hulls. By the sea foods stalls men with windswept hair and pounding heads listened for the mid-day clock to chime the hour. Bolts and locks were turned in unison and for drinkers the day began.

I found out who the mystery Mediterranean protester was when she walked into the Marlow one day. I must have impressed her after all. Her name was Vicky and she worked for a music company. It was a well-paid job that offered the chance of meeting some famous bands. Her boss was over fifty years old. He was inventive, entrepreneurial and desperate to get her into his bed. Vicky took to visiting me regularly and I started to look forward to the London train arriving whenever there was a break in the recording studios. She and the blonde Adonis who had organised the demonstration had been together since university. As he played up to the media, who focused more on his good looks, than his political content, she had begun to see through him. We're all socialists when we're skint. We are all better at receiving than giving. Once we have something to lose though our take on life changes.

A screaming noise woke me up. Something was shrieking from a deep primeval place. Vicky pushed me away from her onto the floor. "Get up. Jimmy Dawes is killing Mary." By the sound of the screams it was too late. "I'm not going up there."I said. "friendship only goes so far. I sat on the edge of the low bed searching for my pants and my solid Spanish boots. I dressed and eased open the door. I could hear breathing and soft sobbing from the top of the stairs. Jimmy Dawes was a dangerous man. He was over six foot tall and had a keen sense of himself. If you fucked with Jimmy you usually lost and if you didn't he would pull in most of his mates to ensure you did the next time. "Perhaps she deserves it," I said quietly closing the door. The banging and the screaming began again. "You go." I suggested. He'll be less likely to beat you up." She pulled on her jeans and a floppy tee shirt.

"Put your boots on." I advised.

"I can run faster bare foot." said Vicky.

The banging continued and a low growling noise could be heard beneath the soprano screams. We bounded up the stairs to stop the mayhem. Jimmy Dawes was naked, holding on to the door knob with both hands, he was leaning back with his legs splayed and his feet braced hard against the frame. He was bashed and scratched and terrified. The door finally caved in as a fire grate broke through the plywood paneling to reveal a naked, crazy Mary. Her eyes were fierce and wild, her lips dripping with spittle. Jimmy jumped up and grabbed onto Vicky, using her as a shield he edged his way down the stairs to our flat. "Next time you hear that woman in distress,"I said, slamming and locking the door, "don't call me. Call a psychiatrist." I threw Jimmy a blanket to cover himself. Wrapped up he looked like a bearded Indian warrior back from a battle he had lost.

"I'll go up and see to Mary." said Vicky.

Jimmy looked at me waiting for the first word to be spoken. Waiting for the game to begin.

"She's stone mad." said Jimmy "I don't know how Harry put up with her."

"He didn't put up with her for long Jimmy, she threw him out."

"Yeh, well he's better off now." said Jimmy.

"What's up with Mary anyway?" I ask

"You know, women's problems?"

"What PMT?"

"No preg- nan -cy ."Jimmy spelled out.

"Yours?"

 "So she reckons. I can never work out how they know these things."

Jimmy didn't know very much about other people's feelings. Although he was very aware of his own. He would often pontificate about how humane he was, using the strangest of arguments to prove his point. When he was younger, he used to hang around the tourist hotels waiting for an opportunity to steal a car and its contents. When a family arrived, it was ten to one that the driver would open the boot, get the first bit of luggage out and leave the keys hanging from the raised tailgate; the wife or girlfriend rushing ahead empty handed, looking for the nearest toilet. Jimmy would walk forward, shut the boot and drive off with the car and contents. After he had sifted through all the cases, taking only what he wanted, he would take the car back and park it a couple of streets away from the hotel. "Good job it was me that stole that car," he would boast. "I always take them back, sometimes to the front of the hotel. It makes me feel good." As far as criminals went Jimmy thought he was at least thoughtful. "I'm not the sort to trash the car or piss in the suitcases." he would boast, as if this vindicated his behaviour and having a vehicle stolen by him, was somehow a good start to a family's fortnight holiday.

He didn't so much speak as sneer at the world. Two minutes ago he was a shaking wreck, crying and hiding behind a girl. Now he was puffing up with bravado. "You and Harry looking for a job." he asked. Before I could answer he continued. "Come down the club Monday afternoon I might have something for you?" Vicky returned with clothes for Jimmy to wear.

"You bastard." she started, "have you never heard of contraception?"

"Yeh, I've heard of it," said Jimmy, "it's somewhere in the Caribbean."

Marco from the Roma café was the only son of an immigrant Italian couple from Naples. For a revolutionary Marco had quite a bit to lose. He had a furnished two bed roomed flat above the café in the High street. His mother scrimped and saved and did without. She cooked and cleaned for him and gave him every bit of profit the café and several rented flats brought in. His father, a survivor of the slums of Naples, was part of a larger group of businessmen operating throughout the area. He gave Marco money just to keep him out of his activities, telling him that his time would come. Marco was in his early thirties and his time had already gone as far as his father was concerned. Marco dressed in black to hide his weight problem. His dark hair was curly but thinning. He had the look of a fat lazy bastard about him. Marco was a waster and a lover of young girls. Sometimes what he demanded from the experimenting thirteen year olds, for a weekends stay in his flat or a taxi ride to school, was more than could be expected from a seasoned Bangkok bar girl. For all his bravado and political rhetoric, he was just another spoiled, rich kid waiting for his inheritance.

After the demonstration and political rally, he came up with an idea. "Go to Holland and buy some drugs and maybe some porn mags, return to Britain, sell them and use the money to restart the flagging revolution." Naturally Marco was not going to endanger himself in anyway with the smuggling of the contraband. He could have had the whole thing sorted by the Dutch and their Flying Dutchmen flower trucks that were just beginning to make inroads into the British sluggish flower trade. But he was reluctant to pay. He preferred to receive rather than to give as most of his young conquest could attest.

Thinking that the Irish activists were smuggling weapons into Britain from the Continent, the Customs, Police and immigration departments started to take a greater interest in the Channel ports. The Border Agencies stepped up their vigilance and began to stop and searched travellers both leaving and entering the Country. Ronnie Page, just two days out of plaster was sent back to Amsterdam with enough money to pay off the Dutch. He claimed he was stopped leaving Britain, having requested a bump start from a Customs official when his car stalled at passport control. He was interrogated for some hours after a large sum of money was found carefully secreted in a supermarket carrier bag. The Customs officers accused him of planning to import weapons. He quickly admitted that he was only going to Amsterdam to buy some dope and maybe a few girlie magazines. He said they confiscated the money and sent him on his way. That was his story anyway. This upset the Dutch dealers who were still demanding payment after his last disaster. Marco needed somebody to get over there and sort the whole show out. Revolutions need a leader and being the one with the money he nominated himself. In the committee room at the back of the bar Jimmy Dawes sat with Marco at his side. Jimmy's voice hinted sadness even affection as he told us that Ronnie Page had thrown himself over the cliff in full view of an incoming ferry and three Dutch tourists from Amsterdam. The three Dutch tourists did not want to be identified. Ronnie barely could be. The message was accepted for its simplicity - Don't fuck with the Dutch.

When Harry and I got off the ferry at Zeebrugge we turned left and headed up for Amsterdam, all expenses paid, or would be once we returned safely to Britain. The motorway was fast and flat. We arrived in the early evening and drove to the address that we had been given. The order of hashish and a bundle of assorted Dutch literature were parceled and ready for collection. We were simply the couriers. We loaded the gear in the back of the van among the rest of the junk, turned around and headed straight back to the port. Just before dawn we cleared customs in Britain and headed for the rendezvous with Marco at his apartment in the High Street.

Harry enthused about the van and how pleased he was with it. I reminded him that technically it was mine. We were both looking for our pay day. As we rounded into the high street and approached The Roma Café, a following police car turned on its blue light, gave a couple of whoops from the siren, then pulled in behind the van. My hearts sank, and the blood drained from Harry's face. We stayed in the car until the police officers approached. Harry, who was driving, got out. From the front window of his flat Marco checked out the sirens and saw the van being stopped. One policeman was checking Harry's license as the other peered through the windows into the van. I got out and offered to open up the back doors.

"Is this your vehicle?" asked the first policeman.

"No, it's mine." I said, wondering if should say it was the Machine mans.

"We did a spot check on this vehicle sir and the licensing vehicle authorities have no record of it. It does not appear to exist." My nerves started to recover. I realised this was not about what we thought it was about. Harry with great relief explained that the vehicle had been off the road for some years and we had restored it. He showed the police officer the M.O.T. and valid insurance. The new registration had only just been applied for, Harry explained, but he had been assured by the licensing department that the vehicle could still be legally driven. Satisfied with the explanation the police officer issued a docket to bring in the relevant document or a note from the Vehicle Licensing Authority within the week, said goodnight and drove off.

There was no reply when we rang Marco's bell. I tried the door and it opened. We walked into the sitting room carrying the goods. A young girl lay on the couch, she was only about fourteen years old but had long ago stopped being a child.

"Where's Marco?" Harry asked.

The young girl looked up with hardened eyes and nodded towards the hall.

"Hi Marco," shouted Harry suddenly opening the cupboard door "what's the matter?"

"You tell me," whispered Marco.

"Well your fat, scared, suffering from premature baldness and have a liking for everybody's younger sister."

He stepped out of the closet. "What did the police want?"

"A routine check,"

"Are you sure?"

"Nope,"said Harry " we need paying. Here's your shopping."

"You shouldn't have brought that up here. I don't want it in here, get it down to the club. Jimmy will sort it out. The police pull was probably part of a bigger plan. They are out to get some of us after the demo."

"Why would they want to get you? That was weeks ago and you were nowhere to be seen." I said.

"I was there in the background along with the other politicos." boasted Marco.

"Yeah all those who were too scared to show their faces. I came away from the demo with scars, real scars, look the hair still hasn't grown back yet." I boasted.

"I doubt it ever will." said Harry, recognising the start of male pattern baldness. Who's going to pays us?" he demanded of Marco

"Here." Marco pulled out a couple of notes and handed them to Harry. "Get that stuff down the club later. I'll phone Jimmy we'll sort out the cash then."

Marco gave Harry enough cash for a few beers and enough promises for a lifetime. We were now worse off than before the trip started. We loaded the gear back into the van.

"How come we're always last in line for the pay-out? But first in the line when something needs done.?" I asked.

"Some folks need money Ricky, but people like us thrive on experience." said Harry

"You believe that Harry?"

"Nope "said Harry.

"Good," I said. "because I am sick of being at the bottom of the shit heap. We took the van around to the Machine man's yard parked it up and walked home. We were tired. Harry was back at my place temporarily, him and Julie had been having some serious talks about their future. I was too, with Vicky. We agreed to get some sleep and sort out the dope and the club later.

When it was still a genuine working man's club, men and their wives would come in for a drink or two and a game of snooker, darts or bingo. The snooker and darts were still there but the bingo had been replaced by the Machine man's illegal Chicago style one armed bandits. Workers and their wives were scarce on the ground. It had become a flophouse. In the bar men were sprawled around smoking and drinking. A few women, still clinging to their dreams, had brought their children to get a glimpse of a father or some cash for food.

Jimmy felt destined for greater things. He became the treasurer of the club. Voted in by his mates. Once again, the club's safe was stacked with dodgy money. "On account of the recent attempted robbery" he had argued, "it would be shrewder to hide the weekends takings in a box of cheese and onion crisps, rather than in the solid, impossible to shift, steel safe. When Jimmy made his proposal, the committee demanded a vote. He waited till near last orders, before asking for a show of hands. Thinking that they were being offered a free beer, the motion was carried unanimously. Strangely enough someone broke into the club that night and stole the box of crisps.: Fuck me." said Jimmy, when informed the next day. "who could have foreseen that?"

We followed Jimmy Dawes into the filthy back room. "I think I'm going to have to get a new cleaner," he mused, clearing rubbish off the chairs for us to sit on. "I had to sack the last one, she came under suspicion after the robbery."

"Everybody knows it was you who stole the weekends take Jimmy." I pointed out.

"No," said Jimmy. "Some people thought she did it. She had access and opportunity and she was skint. Reasons enough. I had to get rid of her just in case."

"Just in case it wasn't you?" said Harry.

"Justice must be seen to be done." said Jimmy spreading his hands in resignation.

"Funny that." Said Harry, I saw your Tracy cycling along the front on a new bike.

I asked her where she got it. "Jimmy found it" she shouted peddling away like a mad thing. Didn't look cheap to me."

"No, no." That's nothing to do with the robbery" He pointed out. "Naw she won that."

"Eh?" we asked as one.

"Yeah, Christmas raffle, first prize."

"This Christmas coming?" enquired Harry.

"Yeah, but you know what kids are like? Can't wait for Santa.

Jimmy Dawes sat down at the table and took on his official persona. We accepted the beer offered and settled back to await our pay off. "Marco phoned," began Jimmy. "he's panicking. He wants it out of town as soon as possible.

"We just want to be paid." said Harry.

Jimmy shifted in his seat and held his hands in front of him as if in prayer. "Marco's fondness for young girlies is getting too well known. It's embarrassing. The last thing we want is the police stumbling on our new venture before we have time to get it shaped up and professional," said Jimmy. "Marco's got a problem and we can't have the police sniffing about. All it will take is one parent finding out that sweet little Lucy isn't on a stopover with her mates after all; but getting stoned and screwed by their worst nightmare."

"So what's the deal?" Asked Harry.

I'll pay you in hash."

"Fuck that." I said.

"How much?" said Harry.

"Half and I'll keep the magazines. Marco will probably need them where he's going."

"Okay." said Harry.

We handed over the hashish less our share. We

left the club and drove the van with the gear back to the Machine man's yard, parked it up and walked to the Marlow. I was going to phone Vicky in London to see if her recording mates wanted to buy our share, delivered of course.

In the Marlow bar Julie was sitting at a table alone. She turned away when she saw Harry. Something was amiss. Harry ordered two beers and joined Julie. I went into the phone booth in the bar and phoned Vicky in London. Harry guzzled at his beer trying to get some moisture into his dry throat.

"What's happened?" asked Harry.

 "Sandy's got a release date. He'll be out by late February."

"Jesus that's not so good."

"I'm pregnant."Julie said.

"That good?" asked a nervous Harry. "Sandy know?"

"Nope "said Julie.

"Is it his." asked Harry.

"It can only be yours." she replied.

"How?"

Julie looked at Harry and realised that it wasn't only lost Amazonian tribes that made no connection between copulation and pregnancy, it was just about every man she had ever met. "If he finds out it's yours Harry, you're dead." Harry said nothing as Julie left the bar and walked away.

Big Ray light up a cigarette and blew a puff of smoke into the air. "What's up with you.?

"Sandy's getting out in February." said Harry.

"Big trouble Harry. That's only a few months away. I've heard he knows about you and Julie. The Machine man's been keeping him well informed of your activities. He's sited a few of his one-armed bandits in the Prison Officers' Club. You know the ones that're illegal. He says beating you senseless is the only thing that keeps Sandy going, it gives him something to look forward to. If he finds out she's pregnant."

Sandy would soon be out and focused as never before on catching up with his old mate Harry. Although Sandy didn't spend anytime with Julie it was a power thing for him. It wasn't the power over Julie that he enjoyed but the fear he instilled in other men. Few would buy Julie as much as a drink in case the action was misinterpreted by the psycho Scot. Harry had broken that rule. He was going to have to be punished.

At 08.31 hrs. the local C.I.D and drug squad were the first customers into the Café Roma. At 08.33 hrs the police booted in Marco's apartment door in time to witness the fourteen-year-old daughter of a member of the local council kiss another member goodbye. They had been tipped off by an anonymous caller concerned about the goings on in Marco's flat. Jimmy Dawes was nothing if not thorough.

Harry and I met up with Vicky and one of the soundmen at a bar near the recording studio in London. The roadie, a big disheveled Irishman, dipped his nose into the bag containing the sample, snorted like a feeding horse and declared with a smile. "Good gear, got anymore? "I wonder how much hash cost per kilo in Morocco?" mused Harry as we drove back from London. "If I can get some money together and offer Julie a better life, we may have a chance." Harry was in love with Julie. He had to be, to even contemplate getting back together. The aggrieved Sandy was about to come out of jail. I agreed to go with him. We would use the money we had made from the hashish to stake a run to Morocco. If this stuff came from Morocco what were we doing buying it in Holland. It didn't make sense. The smart thing was to go directly to the source. A few kilos of hashish would set us up and out of the area before Sandy was released. The price in Britain was at least ten times the cost in Morocco, explained the excited Harry as he worked out the expected profit. His revolutionary tendencies were weakening in the face of easy money. This could be the start of something big for him and Julie. If she took him back they could move to Scotland and buy a cottage. He had heard that they could be renovated for next to nothing in remote areas. And remote is what he wanted.

Harry spent a couple of days servicing the van. He built a false bulkhead behind the spare wheel. It was late November; our business was about to expand. The only thing of interest apart from the scenery on the cold trip down through France and Spain was that I was run over. We had a puncture and Harry was changing the wheel by the roadside in a village on the route South. I did what I always did when Harry started working on a problem. I looked for a bar. I spotted one on the other side of the road and walked out in front of what appeared to be a corrugated iron box on wheels. I bounced off the bonnet and into the bar. The astonished driver stopped the car and rushed into the café, where he found me ordering two small beers. I didn't seem damaged and another dent on the battered old motor would hardly affect its sale price. He was relieved and ordered a double Pastis for himself and insisted on paying for the round. We had a couple of drinks at his expense and said farewell to our newfound friend and commented on the friendliness of the natives. We were on the Abbeyville to Paris road and passed a sign for Agincourt.

"France is a great country, loads of history." I said to Harry. "Strange how the English have this, we're better than you are attitude towards them." "That's cause the men are all effete and the women lust over a bit of prime roast beef." He replied, rubbing his genitals. Not like Harry I thought, we must be pissed. We stopped for a break in Agincourt and wandered through the town to shape up a bit. Harry picked up a guide book. " Ahh." He revealed beginning to read the brochure. "The reason we think the Frenchies are lower beings than us? It's a left over from the recent battle of 'Agincourt', 600 odd years ago. It was a victory for the English and Welsh longbow archers." Despite them dying where they stood from dysentery, the archers could still flick the old fuck off 'V' sign. Even though they were shitting their lives out of their arse, they still had two fingers to deal with the foppish French. Give him his due Henry Vth was there, or so his official report claimed. Charles VI wasn't, he was home in bed unwell. An endorsement of the Englishmen's opinion of their enemy. Later Henry took Charles's daughter as part payment for his victory. Just a family squabble. They were all closely related and loved each other really". "You've made half of that up" I said. "Come on let's find a bar. I'm starting to feel a thirst coming on."

Each day we drank as we drove, until neither of us was fit to continue, then we pulled off at a bar for a few beers before sleeping in the vehicle. We had decided to avoid the motorways because we objected to paying the auto route charges. What we saved on tolls, our logic told us, was spare money and like all spare cash we spent it on drink. We crossed the border into Spain away from France's 'Liberty Equality and Fraternity' and into "Franco land." General Franco was still alive. He had reached the top of the tree in Fascist Spain. He treated all those who thought a little different from himself the same… He had them shot. Thousands of them. We soon found out that beer and wine were dirt cheap and fags were almost free. "Franco might be a bit of a bastard." I said. "But he knows what the working poor want." Spain passed in a blur of fatigue and cheap Brandy.

Part 2.

MINT TEA IN MOROCCO.

I awoke in the back of the van. My head ached from a nights drinking in Cueta the Spanish duty free port in Morocco. North African music blared out of an open shutter. A shout sent out the same message everywhere on Earth, when the young play their thoughts too loud, "For the love of Allah turn that fucking shite down". In Arabic of course. "Who am I? where am I? and what am I doing here?" I yawned, looking out of the back windows of the van at a village struggling into early morning life. "This must be Morocco. When did we get here, who drove?"
"I don't remember," said Harry.

The street in front was shaking back to life. A café opened and a young man carelessly brushed the walkway in front of the run-down establishment. We tumbled out of the van, walked across the empty street and entered the café through a beaded door. There were a couple of tables and folding chairs and not much else. The young man had vanished. The kitchen area was divided from the dining space by a curtain. On the floor on a shakedown we found the youth back in bed, huddled under an old coat. Harry shook him, he seemed unimpressed with his early morning clientele. He assured us that we could have coffee just as soon as he got up and would not be offended if someone put the water on. I lit the gas ring and ran the tap for a while before filling a pot with water. The youth started to cough and choke like a cat. He balanced his racking frame on the edge of the shakedown and took out a little pipe and filled it with greenery. He lights it and drew in, forcing down the healing smoke, his coughing fit subsided and he moved from the bed to the table where Harry was already sitting. "What about mint tea? Harry asked "mint tea in Morocco, isn't that famous?"

"I know nothing of that," he replied "I am a student."

With a short burst of air from his re-inflated lungs the student cleared the pipe bowl of ash and debris. It landed accurately onto the table. He filled it again and offered the pipe to Harry. The young café worker had found a friend in Harry. Common interest always beats reality. The water was boiling. Harry sucked deeply on the contents of the one draw pipe.

"What do I do next," I asked.

The young man looked up with tar black eyes and filled the pipe again.

"Open the jar," he advised "one spoon per cup then fill with water."

He seemed amazed that I had never experienced the joys of instant coffee granules. We sat at the table in silence, our hangovers retreating as the marijuana took effect. We sipped on mugs of muddy coffee. The warming sun beamed in through the open door. Buses roared up and slammed to a halt outside the café. Moroccan women and school children squabbled to board before the vehicles sped off in a whirl of diesel and dust. As the village rush hour reached its peak, pedestrians shouted abuse at the drivers who raced to keep to their schedules. Lorries, vans and donkeys, swayed and swerved up and down the road at random. The coffee cooled and time passed.

A cat was highlighted in the doorway. The cat came towards us its back legs not following the front. It seemed to be having a problem balancing. "What happened to that cat?" asked Harry.
"It just go like that," said the student.

A poster in the café promoted Morocco. Land of sun, sea, sandy beaches, street traders, the mighty ocean, couscous, snake charmers; the gateway to Africa. Berber women in colourful clothes and tattooed faces smiled alongside teenage girls in bikinis and tight designer swimsuits. The older dignified parents and grandparents in traditional dress smiling at the near nakedness of the young. "I can't wait to see them slip off their djellabas." I said, pointing out the poster. Harry ignored me. He was more concerned about the cat than my fantasies. "Rabies," said Harry "I saw a programme on the television just before we left. I think that cat's got rabies. The first thing that goes is the motor nerves."

"I thought it was water. Don't they get an aversion to water?"

"Only at the very end." said Harry watching the cat. "That's when everybody can tell."

The cat advanced towards the table making strange baby like noises.

"It's going mad," he said, slowly edging his chair to the opposite side of the room.

"How do you know? That could be cat Arabic." I said trying to lighten up the situation. "I reckon it's been run over."

"Well I'm not taking any chances," said Harry. "Let's find the campsite. It'll be safer."

Harry rose from the table and backed towards the door.

"How much for the coffee?" he asked. The student fixed him with eyes that could see through a wallet and quoted a price that would not be out of place in top London restaurant.

"What?" said Harry "I could buy five jars of coffee for that price in Britain."

"Yes, me too." said the student. "maybe more.

Okay I will take off the service charge, no service charge today?"

"I made the coffee," I said. "I served you."

"Give him the money." said a resigned Harry heading for the door. I handed over the cash. Lying outside on the walkway was a large dog that had appeared from nowhere and had fallen into a troubled sleep.

"The dog's got it too" said Harry "it's having a convulsive fit the very last stages. Let's get out of here. We're slap bang in the middle of a rabies outbreak." The student came to the door. "My brother comes back today, this is his café. I find you at the camping and take you to see my friends."

"Okay," Harry shouted as he ran for the van.

The campsite wasn't busy. Neither of us had erected a tent before. Compared to the elaborate desert style dwellings spaced around the site, our dull green four berth arctic tundra shelter was basic. Taking it out of the bag had us both sweating. We could hear the chuckles of mirth from the most famous tent dwellers on earth as we fussed and fought to spread out our tiny canvas home. Jimmy Dawes had claimed that the tent was in good order and fit for action when he loaned it to us as his contribution to the venture. It was apparent that some of the important bits like poles and guy ropes were missing. I crawled into the interior of the tent and stood up. "If we can improvise a pole here and there, we may be able to get this thing looking like a tepee." I said. On closer inspection the tent walls seemed to be splattered with blood and dried vomit and what looked like a pair of soiled tights. That decided the accommodation problem. "I don't think there is any need for a tent." I said. "We should just sleep in the van."

We abandoned the tent and went to the café bar on the campsite for an omelette. An American family were eating doughnuts and drinking cola at the café, enjoying the late autumn sun; their young children playing with a scruffy campsite puppy dog. Harry warned the parents about the outbreak of rabies in the area. The baffled puppy was shunned and shooed away and the kids put under strict supervision for the rest of the day.

In the afternoon, Mustapha came wandering down to the campsite to meet us. When we explained that we were going to find a beer in the village; he knew just the place. We followed him back to his café. His brother was back, food was being cooked and customers were drinking tea. Harry scanned the area for the rabid cat and dog. Mustapha introduced us to his brother who was called Sallah. Then he went into a chest fridge and brought out two stubby bottles of beer. We sat down at the table.

"How much?" asked Harry before Mustapha could open them.

"On the house." said Sallah.

"You speak good English." said Harry. "Have you been to England?"

 "Yes "replied Sallah." "In London until the hot season, then up country to the mountains at Manchester." Harry decided not to pursue the conversation.

As soon as the men started to speak there was a movement from the shakedown bed and the cat appeared from behind the dividing curtain. It recognised its old mate Harry and dragged itself towards him. The big dog lumbered into the shade of the doorway and flopped down as if poleaxed and was asleep almost instantly. "For fuck sakes they're back," Harry panicked. He made towards the door but the big old dog jumped up in fear at the sudden movement and growled like a bear. The cat moved in closer. Sallah laughed. "You are afraid of animals?"

"When they have rabies, I am" said Harry

"Rabies?"

"Yes there's an outbreak of rabies. I saw it on the television. That cat is dragging its legs, its motor nerves have gone, a sure sign."

"I expect they have" said Sallah the cat was run over by the school bus in the summer. She is fine now. And the dog, he just sleeps all day wherever he wants he is older than me I'm sure." Mustapha was setting up his pipe and laughing. "You should take a little more mint tea with your marijuana my friend".

After the beer and a couple of pipes, we left with Mustapha to have a look around the small village. We found a shop that sold red wine in unlabelled bottles. We bought a couple of bottles. The shopkeeper wrapped them in newspaper and advised secrecy. He explained that it was illegal to drink the stuff in public, but we could consume the wine in the back of his shop. It seemed strange. On a bench in front of the shop a couple of men were happily puffing away on their hash pipes yet we had to smuggle our contraband wine back to the café. Mustapha told us that it would be okay to drink it in his brother's bar. He assured us that there would only be a nominal charge for corkage. We were beginning to like Mustapha.

By late afternoon, shops, cafes and stalls had set up griddles and barbecues in the streets to cater for the last of the tourists. People came out of their houses to enjoy the cool evening and the campers came up from the beaches. Kebabs were sizzling above expertly fanned fires. Lamps were lit and the place bustled to the music of the street. That evening we dined well from Sallah's kebab stall and sat happily outside the café smoking and drinking the rough red wine. I was amused by the contradiction of cultures.

The men of the village seemed happy and content to sit around nursing soft drinks and smoking marijuana in their mini pipes. There was no aggression, no threatening behaviour. The only people who looked like they might get out of control were Harry and me smashed on a cocktail of two colliding cultures. "Imagine," began a philosophical Harry "what it would be like if the authorities in Britain stopped the production of alcohol? If the Americans were still into prohibition and took it upon themselves to police Europe, burning fields of barley and destroying breweries and historic distillers. Old farmers taken out back and shot for growing barley and grapes? Mind you," he reflected looking down at the sour Moroccan red eye. "whoever made this stuff deserves to be shot."

We spoke of travel and freedom of governments and politics. Sallah admitted he had never been to Britain. He had never been anywhere outside the Riff and the coastal plain.

"We are Berbers." He explained "for us travel is difficult, for many impossible. Even if we have money it is not easy to obtain documents. If we are discovered to have forged papers, we will be jailed for being illegal immigrants or part of a terrorist organisation. For us the world is not free and open."

It was agreed that the next day we would go up the mountain with Mustapha and buy a few kilos of hashish. As the evening progressed, the temperature dropped and families returned to the warmth of their houses. By the time we made it back to the van we were both pissed. I insisted on moving the van closer to the toilet block. The rough red wine was burning a hole in my stomach and I knew it would be one of those sudden calls. I had just snuggled into the back of the van, wrapped like a turkey in my moon style silver sleeping bag, when the rumbling of my irritated bowel signalled a flight to salvation. The lights in the toilet block were switched off and I stumbled into one of the cubicles, squatted down over the hole and exploded. I heard someone approaching the toilet. The American men entered the block. I squatted in silence and listened. The smell from my cubicle was overpowering. One of the American men retched. "Jesus," he said. "I have just come back from China and Christ I thought that the toilets smelled bad there. But this place would gag a fucking maggot." They zipped up and left, muttering about dysentery and rabies and just how safe was Morocco anyway? I stood up and felt around for the toilet chain and pulled it. The toilet I was about to find out, was also the shower, or more likely the shower also doubled as a flush toilet. Water flooded down soaking me. I dripped out and staggered back the short distance to the van. Harry stirred. "Is it raining?" he asked somewhere in his dreams. "It's raining," I said drumming my fingers on the roof of the van.

The smiling Mustapha woke us at dawn. He was ready to take us to the area where the marijuana was grown in a patchwork of illegal fields. We paid for our night in the campsite with cash. The money went straight into the pocket of the man who had slept all night guarding the tents. Mustapha insisted that we should get on our way and stop later at a roadside café for a coffee and doughnut breakfast. He elected to sit next to the window insisting that this would ensure safe passage and no harassment. I squeezed in between the two of them. It was important, he explained to have a well-known guide, we were going into Berber territory. Not a place to venture into alone. We drove down from the coastal plain passed the town of Tetouan and followed the road south for a while. Then we turned left and headed up towards the distance mountains. At the junction a police vehicle and a spiked chain, blocked the opposite side of the road. "Only one road down the mountain" said Mustapha.

"How do you get passed that?" asked Harry.

"We pay them."

"Corruption." I said. "The ruination of civilisation."

Mustapha laughed. "You speak from a position of privilege."

I watched the police out of the back window as the roadblock disappeared behind us. We stopped at a roadside shack café. Two men sat outside at a table. Mustapha greeted them. "My cousins," he said. The two men went back to their task of working by hand, the pollen from the buds of the marijuana plants until a sticky resin was formed. An older man brought coffee and doughnuts. Harry offered to pay. "There's no charge," said the man.

Funny how the world is? What's fine in one country is taboo in another. Hashish, thanks to the American 'Beat Writers' and hippies had spread it's cool message to Europe. With the introduction of the Cold Water Press the cannabis pollen could be compressed into manageable blocks. This made concealment for the smugglers easier. Although cannabis had been smoked in the Riff for centuries it had been outlawed by the Moroccan Government after pressure from the United States and Europe.

After the hillside town of Chouen, where only forty years earlier the severed heads of captured soldiers from Franco's army grimaced out a warning to all, there was only one place a vehicle was going, up the twisting torturous route to Ketama. In the summer the green fields of cannabis plants sway gently in the warm mountain breezes, protected from the winds by beautiful Lebanese cedar trees and guarded from thieves by Berber tribesmen with sickles, swords and machine guns. It was dark when we arrived at a ramshackle village. We parked the van off the road and followed Mustapha down a track to a group of huts roofed with corrugated iron. He banged on the door of the largest building. "Hotel" he said to us as he banged again and shouted "Mohammed." The door opened and a young boy peered out. He greeted Mustapha. Then we were led to a room where a man was sleeping on a broken-down bed. Mohammed shouted and shook him awake. The sleeping tribesman stirred from his slumber grumbled into his beard, grabbed a blanket and went out and lay down in the hall. Mohammed quickly tidied up the bed and standing back, proudly offered the accommodation to us. Harry's wits came back first. "How much for the room?" he asked.

"Nothing you are our guest," replied Mustapha.

"This is my home."

The young boy brought us coffee and fresh pressed hashish.

"In the summer," our new friend said, making a pipe. "this place is alive, day and night, supplying kebabs and coca cola for the smugglers and gangsters. But the summer is over and when the snow falls the mountain road will be washed away. We give this to you like apples in a bag." he said holding up a block of freshly presses cannabis resin. "You take it to your country and sell it for many times more that you pay for it here."

"We have to get it home first," said Harry.

When the deal was done, we stacked five kilos of hashish in the false bulkhead behind the spare wheel. In the middle of the night we drove back down the mountain. Mustapha stayed to visit family members. By morning we had made it pass Chouen. There were no police road block at the junction.

We were looking forward to a good breakfast in Cueta. Our passports were stamped and we were waved out of Morocco. The sun was dazzling, reflecting off the Mediterranean Sea like a headlight in a rear view mirror. The dust was rising and billowing, spiralling in the warmth of a Moroccan winter. There were no tourists to blend among, no happy, long haired hippies, no bustle of summer day trippers, only strong legged Moroccan women carrying their inevitable bundles to the daily contraband markets at either side of the border.

I saw the man first. He was reading a newspaper which he folded when he saw the van approach. He straightened up and a smile crossed his face. His wait had been rewarded.

"Fuck," I said. "who is that?"

The man stepped in front of the van. We were funnelled into a warehouse. The double doors were opened as we reached them and closed as we entered. No word was spoken. The grey-haired man indicated to us to leave the vehicle and open up the bonnet and back doors. The inside of the van was strewn with empty bottles and rubbish and a jumble of clothes, half eaten food and Jimmy Dawes' tent. We watched as the elderly man struggled into his overalls. An assistant arrived carrying torches and rods and drills and wires. Tools of their trade. Their trade was to catch drug smugglers. We sat in stunned silence as the two customs officials began their work. We were aware, far too late, that things were about to go wrong. A uniformed customs official arrived and checked our passports and documentation.

After searching for a while the grey-haired man
and his assistant had found nothing. They had
not located the false bulkhead behind the spare
wheel. They stopped their work. As the grey-
haired man rested, the younger assistant left the
garage by a side door. Soon the younger man
returned with a scrap of paper in his hand. He
looked at the piece of paper and then at the
number plate. "Si si" he confirmed. The older
man began again. He took out the spare wheel
and deflated the tyre, he felt around the inner rim
finding nothing. He looked in the litter strewn
vehicle, squatted and looked into the spare
wheel recess. He shone his torch into the
shadow. Then he took out a bamboo stick and
pushed it into the space. He marked the length
with a piece of tape. Then he measured the floor
of the van. A smile flickered on his face, his chin
quivered. He had found a discrepancy; he had
discovered the false bulkhead. He quickly broke
into the cavity and hauled out the five kilos of
hashish. He shook Harry's hand then mine. He
seemed delighted. The grey haired man removed
his overalls, checked his watch and smiled at the
prospect of an early lunch.

Dear Ma life's hell sell the pig and buy me out.
Dear Son pig's dead shape up and soldier on.
You can only fuck around with life for so long

before life fucks back.

It was Friday morning and the streets were bustling. A break in the crowd was created by armed policemen. We were escorted from the police van and rushed into the Ceutan police station. We were the first of the weekend visitors to the jailhouse. There were four barred cells, the type that in a television western would have held the town drunks and the misunderstood hero. Three of the cells were in a line together and the fourth was set back around a corner and just out of eyeshot from the others. "We'll probably get a small fine and be home in a few days." I said.

"This is serious," said Harry

"It's your cheerfulness that keeps you going isn't it? The stuff's almost legal in Morocco."

"We're not in Morocco, this is Cueta, Spanish territory." answered Harry.

"Same thing."

"No its not." said Harry "Spain has a tough policy on drugs, a tough policy on everything."

By late afternoon we realised that nothing was coming our way in the form of food or drink. Harry shouted for the guard. The guard, a fat man, arrived and explained in simple Spanish and hand signs that we could buy whatever we wanted. He took our order and disappeared. He returned with two ham baguettes and a beer each. It seemed that all might not be lost. Harry paid. Later I asked for a cigarette. The jolly man went off and came back with a pack of twenty. The charge was the same. It dawned on us that a weekend in the cells in Cueta was different to the solitude of the British penal system. We ordered a few more bottles of beer and settled down to wait. There was a concrete block bed, a thin blanket and nothing else in the cell. In the early evening a drunken, shaven headed Moroccan was dragged into the jail, kicking and muttering. He laid where he was thrown and fell asleep. Harry and I took turns dozing on the concrete bed. At first the filthy blanket was discarded. Then as the temperature plummeted, we were begging and bribing for another. It was late into the night when the bulk of the inmates arrived. Six girls heavily made up, high-heel booted and mini-skirted. They were put into the cell next to the Moroccan who was wakened by the commotion. The guard took the big man out of his cell and put him in with me and Harry. He immediately occupied the bed block and moaning like a wounded bear, draped the stained blanket around his head and declared in English that he was Dadi, from Ketama, a Berber not Moroccan and that Cueta belonged to him and not the fucking Spanish.

Then he fell back to sleep. Three of the girls were put into Dadi's vacant cell. The lights were dimmed. Within the hour the first of many visitors appeared. He chose the girl he wanted and after paying the smiling jailor, took her into the vacant cell. A bit of grunting and groaning and they were done. This went on for half the night. Different men appeared paid the piper and called the tune. Before morning the six girls had gone. Dadi was moved back into his own cell where he sat like an angry Buddha. He spoke English well and smoked most of our cigarettes. He explained that we would all be going to P. P. Rosales for a while.

On Monday morning the guards arrived to escort us to court. Apart from few of kilos of quality hashish, what did they have? Easy pickings we soon discovered. The delousing centre was adjacent to the court. The guards un-cuffed Dadi, Harry and myself and left us at the entrance to a concrete shower block. The man in charge told us to strip and put our clothes into a fumigation box. The showers were switched on, a long run of them. The scalding water steamed out. We dashed through trying to avoid the hot jets, our skins glowed like ripe tomatoes. The man who ran this facility was himself a prisoner. He was a dark Spaniard with blue, oiled hair, styled and quiffed like a cowboy rock and roller. Harry sat naked on the barber's chair, hair and beard shaved off, one side only. A before and after mug-shot, captured in an instant of time. The barber first turned Harry's head one way, then the other. A happy, carefree hippie, from one view; a sinister looking skin head convict from the other. With a turn of the head and a scrape of the razor, our lives were transformed.

A desk of military men, outshone by their medals sat in front of us. Papers were shown, and pages were signed. We were escorted into the holding room and once again handcuffed to Dadi. The big Moroccan sat, head down, eyes fixed on something in his mind. We were loaded into the back of the prison van and driven out to P. P. Rosales. The letters P. P. in front of Rosales stand for Prison Penitentiary. We strained to see out of the vehicle as it approached the solid green doors, painted and repainted by soldiers, sailors, drifters, bums, small time crooks, bandits and tearful bankrupts. The big gates were opened and we disembarked into a courtyard and shuffled through a second set of doors and up to a circular glass reception area. The floor was tiled and gleaming. The police escort un-cuffed us and handed us over to be processed. Harry and I were dealt with by a warder who spoke English. Dadi was escorted into another part of the prison. There were no regulation prison clothes.

Our money and passports were handed over to the prison warder by the escort guard. The money would be held at the reception area and could be changed at anytime for low denomination prison currency tokens. We had around two hundred pounds between us enough for the journey home. Rosales was going to be a cheap place to over winter, if our tastes stayed simple. The prison guard shouted to a youth, a runner who was sitting awaiting orders. We followed him up a stairway. At the top was a landing and two large cell blocks. They were adjacent to each other. One was for the Europeans and the other for the North Africans. The youth introduced himself as Hans from Holland. "This is our Brigada," he said in English. The Brigada was an oblong room with an open barred frontage looking out onto a landing, at the far end of which was the Moroccan Brigada. Numbed, we scanned the cell. The bunks were arranged around the wall. The only light came from the barred windows. It was cold and damp. Hans indicated an empty bunk. It was next to the toilet. The toilet was a hole in the ground with a rusted can of water to clean whatever needed cleaning. Thin, stained mattresses sagged through the few strands of wire that had not been cannibalised for other beds. This space was reserved for the new boys. "When somebody is released from the Brigada, you will get a better position." Hans explained.

"Shift up a notch and this dismal corner would be the province of another, just caught, sad, lost soul," I muttered.

We threw down our bags and followed the Dutchman back down the steps to join the other foreign prisoners. The yard was cobbled and shiny from feet going nowhere. Small groups huddled in corners with coats and blankets covering their heads. One or two men marched up and down military style attempting to keep warm. The winter sun had still not reached this part of the planet. The building was designed for maximum summer shade. Heat escaped through the top of my shaven head. I hunched my shoulders and moved into the courtyard.

To the right was a covered walkway that lead to an eating area. A large wooden trestle table and two benches were the only furnishings. If it rained the walkway and the dining room would be the only places to shelter. At the bottom of the walkway and past the canteen the toilet block was situated. Six holes in the ground side by side. We had arrived in time for the only hot meal of the day. Hans took us through the procedure. We were given our only prison possessions, an aluminium bowl and a spoon. Before the meal we lined up with the others waiting for the prison shop to open. It opened twice a day, at noon and then again at six in the evening. The shop supplied essentials, stamps, cards, toothpaste, sweets, cigarettes. And, most importantly, wine. The authorities, aware that most behaviour problems were caused by alcohol depravation allowed wine twice a day. A large tumbler of sour red wine costing almost nothing, was administered at noon and at then again at six in the evening. We could buy as many cigarettes as we wanted. A packet as cheap in jail as out, making trading in tobacco, pointless. The prison authorities didn't condone the use of drugs but ignored the smoking of hash. It was cheap and readily available from the Moroccans. I choked down the vinegar wine and followed the Dutchman back into the yard and across to the eating area. As we re-entered the yard, a small tough looking man wearing a military style coat was holding out his aluminium bowl like a beggar on the streets. He laughed with bleary eyes as a tall youth in cowboy boots and a long black coat walked up to him and emptied the contents of his mouth into the awaiting bowl. The man swallowed the frothy wine, with one gulp. "Legionnaires." said Hans.

We congregated with the others milling around the eating area. Two prisoner orderlies brought the food. Bread, oranges, a box of salted sardines and a large metal urn. They took great care not to disturb the contents of the urn. They placed the container on the trestle table. A dapper man dressed in flannels, a blazer and a pair of old baseball boots arrived to serve the food. "Carlos," informed Hans. "he thinks he runs the place."

Walking alongside Carlos, like a psychopathic presidential bodyguard, was his minder.

" Casablanca," the Dutchman whispered "he chopped up two French girls."

"Why?" I enquired.

"Perhaps you should ask him," replied the Dutchman. Casablanca stared at me until I became uneasy. Then he smiled.

We were pushed to the front of the queue and soon found out why. The baseball booted Spaniard began to serve up the food. The ladle skimmed the surface of the soup. We were dished up a bowl of grey water, handed a baguette a sardine and an orange. A well established hierarchy was in existence. Soup wise we were at the top. With luck maybe we could make it to the bottom, where the nutrition was. After the meal there was nowhere to go and nothing to do except pace the yard with Hans who explained the prison set up. The Dutchman was thin and had wispy blonde hair.

He had already been in Rosales for a while and was awaiting transfer to one of the mainland prisons to begin a long sentence. He had married a Moroccan girl and planned to make his fortune running hashish back to Holland. The girl's father had set him up with the first shipment and promptly passed his details on to the customs officers. An ideal way to get rid of an unwanted son-in-law.

The European prisoners were the proof that the Authorities were dealing with the drug problem. Catch the small fish, put them away with large fines and long sentences. Figures don't lie. A conviction is a conviction in the eyes of a statistician, ten grams or ten tons, smuggling is smuggling. The professional traffickers rarely entered Rosales, smuggling being as important to the Cuetan economy as fishing or tourism. The authorised criminals had the freedom to earn the money required for their big houses, fast cars and generous bribes.

Rosales was used as a holding jail for the Europeans. Most bought themselves out, their contributions an essential part of the prison economy. We assumed that we would be freed in a couple of days. Hans agreed. He reckoned that if we could get the money sent from home to pay our fine and a bribe or two and it wasn't held up for weeks or lost in the Spanish banking system, then we could be out in no time. If not it would be an ideal opportunity to learn the Spanish language.

By about three o'clock in the afternoon a slither of warm sunlight shone into the far corner of the dank yard. Taller prisoners were the first to brighten up. Within the hour we crammed into the corner with the others, struggling like fading stars desperate for some of the limelight. In the European Brigada, there were fourteen double bunks. Every time there was a spare bunk another person would be arrested at the customs post. A prisoner's tip: before going through the customs at Ceuta, make a phone call to an inmate of P. P. Rosales and ask about the accommodation situation. If the Brigada is full, load up with high grade zero zero hashish and breeze through customs, puffing on a joint. However if there are a few beds spare, head back to the safety of no-man's land and park up by the beach for a while.

The guard rattled the barred cage. I awoke in the freezing jail. It was relief to get out of the sagging bunk. The cell door was unlocked and I was the first to the stone sinks in the hall. I washed in ice cold water. Breakfast was a sweet cocoa drink and stale bread. We were lined up in the yard and counted, then dismissed. Those important enough, mainly the local Ceutans set off for their privileged, created positions. The rest were set to cleaning up the jail. Most Europeans paid the few pesetas required to sell on their allocated work to the young Moroccans. Harry and I wanted to work. We stood in line with a mop each. Three young Moroccans arrived with a wooden tub full of hot water and a pile of floor cloths. One supervised as the other two dipped the cloths into the hot water, wrung them out and handed them to the prisoners who attached them to brushes and mops. This cloth rinsing had an obvious, coveted perk, warm hands.

Dadi the big Buddha Moroccan walked up to the tub. He removed the three youths with a look that didn't take a Zen philosopher to interpret. He nodded to Harry and me to step forward. We plunged our cold hands into the hot soapy water and began our new job with vigour. When the work was finished, Dadi took us through to the Moroccan yard and we watched in amazement at the industry going on. In the European court the men walked up and down and round and round, dreaming all day of home. Yet in the other yard the air was filled with the aroma of lamb kebabs and couscous. Cooking was an art form here, a restaurant experience unknown to most.

The Moroccan hill men could prepare full meals

on a stove made out of two tin cans. A feat of ingenuity that produced soup, stews, kebabs and tea. Selling tea to the Europeans was a coveted concession. Whoever had the franchise wandered between the yards all afternoon with hot black tea from a thermos. The younger prisoners, and some looked like children, had jobs weaving baskets in the prison workshop. Content with a bed and free food, they saved their slave wages, until their release day. Many of the older men came and went every couple of months. Their crime being to enter the enclave illegally. They were part of a two-way trade, bringing hashish down the mountain and returning with duty free contraband, cigarettes and alcohol. They could rarely resist the temptation to have a few duty free drinks, get drunk and get arrested. They had food and other useful items to trade or sell, brought into the jail by their families. They sold the food they cooked and generally passed their time as profitably as possible. For them the prison was a lucrative place of employment. Their businesses were fiercely protected and continued after their release by other incarcerated family members. They were the people to see about a coat or a jacket, a blanket, food or hashish. For them the jail was a regular trading post.

On Saturdays, a bored, captive clientele puffed away on marijuana and shifted restlessly on hard wooden benches watching General Franco's weekly address to the nation. Franco was wheeled on to the television so that all could see him still alive and in control of the country. He was very old and he looked like a corpse. The prisoners speculated about Franco's death and wondered how long the old dictator could survive. He had been in power since the end of the Spanish Civil War in 1939 and was now in his 83rd year. There was talk that come his demise, there would be an amnesty for all. Why a man, who had never shown any mercy in his life, would soften with death was never fully explained. Some thought him already dead, the weekly apparition a ploy until a new regime could be put into place. Spain was going from military dictatorship to democracy. There was going to be much adjusting. After Franco's address to the nation, us prisoners settled down to watch a bullfight, a football match or a badly dubbed John Wayne movie. Dadi became our link with the Moroccan yard. He had been in and out of Rosales many times. He liked us and we became his fiercely guarded customers. He sold us hashish and shared some of his provisions brought in by his devoted family. He explained that there were well established routes for the drug traffickers to get their product to market. We had chosen the most dangerous. Children earned money by sitting at the side of the road to Ketama taking down foreign vehicle registration numbers and selling them to the police.

We had been in Rosales for nearly two weeks when we were called to the visitors' cell. The British consul was a tall, smart, articulate English speaking Spaniard. He wore thick black glasses and his hair was swept back and oiled. He introduced himself as Senor Rodriguez and handed us a carton of cigarettes each, and a couple of books from the children's classics series, Robinson Crusoe and Kidnapped. I wondered about his sense of humour. He explained that he had paid for and erected signs on both sides of the border, warning of the severe penalties for drug smuggling. We hadn't noticed them. He lectured us about the gravity of our position. How dope made people dopey, and how the jackal only went after the weak, the slow and the confused. We agreed with all he said. We stood in silence, hearing, but not taking in what the consul was saying. "What do we have to do?" Harry asked his voice quivering.

"Have you got any money?"

"No," we replied almost together.

"Do you know anybody who has?"

"Maybe," I said.

"You have only one thing in your favour," he explained, 'Corruption.' Corruption is something that most people condemn as an unfair tool of the wealthy. Well, here you are wealthy." He spoke quietly as he explained how the system worked and the steps to be taken to secure our freedom. "One of you must take the blame for the hashish. The other must deny all knowledge of it. Otherwise you will both be fined for the contraband which if cannot be paid will result in you both being held in jail for three years."

"Three years." I gasped.

"About that," replied the Consul " but you have another charge to answer. The serious offences against public health and order. The prosecutor will push for fifteen years."

"Fifteen years?" I smiled and tried to correct his English. I explained the difference between days, weeks, months and years. The Consul was adamant. "Fifteen years. Unless we can get you out before you go to trial. But it will cost." We were shocked, unbelieving. I saw the colour drain from Harry's face again. "Is that on top of the three years or alongside?" he asked.

"Does it matter? If you cannot get out you will be transferred to the mainland for at least eight years that is with remission." the Consul paused, "If you survive."

"So what is the deal?" asked Harry. "Whoever takes the blame will remain. While the other returns to Britain and raises the money required to get the other out and never to return to any Spanish territory for at least thirty years. Time is running out. Think about it. I can help you, but only as long as you are held here in Rosales. I will have no influence if you are sent to mainland Spain." He pressed the bell and a guard let him out of the visitors' cell.

We joined the queue for our mid-day wine. I had started to participate in the gambling games that some of the prisoners played daily for each other's wine quota. The losers spitting out their ration into the bowl of the winner. Whoever won wandered the yard dazed and content for the rest of the day. Harry had no part of it. He was disgusted. He was also disgusted by the toilet facilities in the yard. Six holes side by side in a corner used by both the Moroccans and the Europeans. Each hole overflowing by mid-morning. Six prisoners squatting whilst another six waited. The cat sized rats startled by the morning activity bounding out between spread legs. Their matted black coats spiked and glistening from the putrid waste. There was no toilet paper just water in a well used can. Paper of any description was hoarded. The Moroccans used water to clean themselves and before long so did I. Harry never used the yard facilities. It was acceptable to urinate in the single hole that served as the Brigada's night toilet facility but it was taboo to shit in it. Harry waited until the middle of the night before crouching in the darkness, hoping the smell would be dispersed come the morning. The alcove that housed the crude plumbing had a barred window that ventilated the room. It was through this opening that the only sight of the outside world could be glimpsed. We took turns peering out at people walking in the streets going about their lives. The ramshackle homes housed Cueta's poorest,. The squats and makeshift huts were the homes of down and outs, illegal immigrants and the families of many who were incarcerated in Rosales.

Christmas was approaching and Harry and I had a decision to make. Who was going to go and who was going to stay? There had been no contact with home. Neither Julie nor Vicky could know how the trip was going. They had no way of finding out. We both needed extra food. To rely on the daily bowl of watery potato soup a sardine or boiled egg and the daily baguette would have us as thin as a blade of grass in months. We were already losing weight rapidly. I thought that I could survive in Rosales better than Harry. Harry was stronger in many ways than me but not when it came to living in a room with twenty eight other halfwits. Besides the van was registered in my name. I was sure that Harry would get me out. I wasn't so sure if I had the same determination to see things through. I would probably let Harry rot. Despite any good intentions I had, I knew that something would crop up to distract me from the task. We were called back to the visitors' cell the next morning.

I thought we could get the Consul to flip a coin or something," said Harry

"No," I said. "the van is registered in my name I can't pretend that you built the compartment without me knowing. Besides Harry, if you get out you will get me out. Whereas I'm not so sure I would be so dedicated. This way we may both get home." Harry began to laugh as we entered the visitors' cell. For all my selfishness it looked like I was about to redeem myself. There didn't appear to be an obvious angle. P. P. Rosales was not the sort of place that many would want to over winter in.

"If I get out, I'll get you out." Harry assured me. We stood awaiting the Consul in silence. The visiting room was no more than a cage. The Consul arrived and spoke to us through the bars. A strong aroma of scented soap and aftershave wafted from him. Harry and myself smelled of Rosales. A heavy, dank, fetid odour of unwashed, slept in clothes. Everything had taken on a dull crumpled greyness. Showers were cold and expensive. There were stories of a washing machine somewhere but we had not seen it. A shave was a weekly event on the day of inspection.

The duty guard wandering past to see if there was any body truly disgusting but standards were low. The Consul kept his distance. "Right," he began at once, "the papers that you signed at the tribunal?"

"Yes," we spoke as one.

"Why did you sign them?"

"They told us to," said Harry.

"Oh you understand Spanish? You both signed an admission of guilt. I have argued that they must be signed again after an interpreter has explained the charges to you. I am that interpreter." The Consul opened a black, scuffed leather attaché case and brought out the relevant paper work. He had marked the sections to be signed. "This is your latest and only hope. It is fortunate that you have landed here at the beginning of the Christmas festivities. The presiding judge is from Cadiz. He is a man with no liking for drugs or drug traffickers. He has gone on his winter vacation. He will not be back until February. His deputy who will stand in for him is a friend of mine and I have already explained your situation. He has agreed that if you both sign a statement, one accepting full responsibility then the other will be released. Then if the fine for the contraband is paid and the bail is accepted for offences against health and public order the other will be set free. The other must wait here with fingers crossed for the money to come through. The judge has also indicated that his wife has spotted a small but expensive set of earrings.

He would like you to buy them for her."

"So what is the total cash I have to come up with to get Ricky out?" enquired Harry.

"Just under three thousand pounds."

"Christ." said Harry , "I could buy a flat for that."

"Yes." replied the Consul thoughtfully "one thing, this is a dangerous time in Spain. Do not become involved in any prison politics. I have to get you out before the end of February, because after then I cannot help. Keep your heads down and your mouths shut."

There was nothing much for Harry to pack up. He searched through the cleanest of his dirty clothes to wear on his journey home. We had signed the papers and within two days the Consul informed Harry of his release date. He was to be given a foot passenger ferry ticket from Cueta to Algeciras in Spain and then a third class train ticket to London. That was it; the best the Consul could do. I sat on Harry's bunk and watched him. "I'm taking a fucking big gamble on you Harry."

"I know." he said. "any ideas how I can get the three grand?"

"Not really. Not my family, they may be able to come up with something, but not three thousand pounds. Leave that as a last resort."

"Vicky, she seems to like you, maybe she can borrow something from her boss."

"Worth a try," I agreed.

"Big Ray?" suggested Harry.

"He's in enough shit of his own. Get in touch with Jack Nunn he owes me from way back."

"What fairy Jack?"

"Yes fairy Jack, he may be able to chip in. He's always liked me."

A few days before Christmas, Harry was released. I watched as he was escorted to recover his few personal possessions from the reception area. Harry looked back toward the yard and shouted, "I won't forget you Ricky. I'll get you out." I sat on the walkway feeling abandoned. I was both pleased and angry. Harry was getting out, that had to be good. Would he get home get the money and get me out? Or would he get home and get stoned and forget about everything. I felt I could handle the Brigada better than Harry. "Born in a caravan in a field next to a building site," he would boast when he wanted to affirm his working-class background. But he didn't like the overcrowded Brigada and the shared exposed toilets. Neither did I. By midday a blanket of despair had cloaked me like a thick woolly mist. I was now truly on my own. The words of the Consulate ringing in his ears. "You best learn Spanish."

Paddy Murphy and Sandy had settled into prison life in Britain. There were enough young thugs from their adopted town to hold them in high esteem. Paddy didn't like hashish or the people who smoked it. One evening during association, he beat up of a couple of hippie prisoners and out of curiosity ate what they were smoking. He swallowed the lump of brown stuff and walked to the recreation area and sat in the villains' corner with Sandy MacLean. Half an hour later Paddy's world changed. He felt strange, as if he was floating, he was gliding towards the toilets when he vomited. His face drained until as white as fear, his hands trembled and his body swayed on jellied legs. His mind raced to gain control, something was happening to him and he didn't know what it was. His survival instinct took over. He flung open the toilet door and settled easily into the gutter of the prison utility urinal. And there he lay undisturbed. Considerate cons pissed around him, while those with an old Paddy inflicted wound or grievance pissed all over him. A smile appeared on his face as the ingested drug took hold and his belief in God and angels, lost since childhood, returned. Paddy Murphy had six months added to his sentence and was transferred to another prison.

Paddy and Sandy were dependant on each other. Together they create a merged single persona. A monster maybe. Sandy was the jaws of the beast but Paddy was the body.

Within a short time of being away from Sandy, Paddy attacked and nearly killed another inmate. He didn't' know why. The prison authorities did. They extended his sentence yet again and he was reclassified as a danger to himself and others. He was going to be away for a while.

Julia agreed to visit Sandy MacLean and was surprised at the change in his appearance. A year in jail, a year off the booze had Sandy looking slimmer, younger and fitter. His unkempt hair had been trimmed, he resembled more an interesting captain of a cruise liner than the dangerous disheveled pirate she remembered. There was something about him that could always breakthrough through her guard. "We can get back together Julie, move back to Scotland, away from everybody. Just you, me and Shona"

"We had something once." Said Julie.

"All the more reason to try again," said Sandy softly.

"Rent a cottage on the edge of a dream? How long before you leave us, how long before the drinking and the fighting and the not knowing?"

"Is it him, do you love him?" asked Sandy, "do

you love Harry?

"I don't know. I like him."

"Did you ever love me?"

"I did Sandy. I really did. But it's a fear thing now. And fear kills love."

"Tell Harry I'll be seeing him, Tell him I'll be looking for him." he said as cold as a sudden frost. Julie rose from her chair and looked at Sandy. "I'm going back home, back to Scotland, back to my family," She leaned over and kissed his cheek, "Bye Sandy. If you could stay the way you are now, we may have a chance. But I know once you are out, it will all start again. Why have you got to hurt Harry?" "Nothing personal," he growled. "Just have to."

Sandy had kept his mouth shut, shaped up, screwed the nut and earned his remission. He was rarely emotional. Years of lying in sweat and shit, in jungles and deserts not knowing where he was and not caring either just as long as at some point the drinks arrived, had left him conditioned to his fate. A soldier, a policeman, a prison warden they were all doing the same thing, just a job, a way to feed the kids, pay the rent get a few beers and beat the tedium and boredom of the daily grind. Sandy felt no hatred towards the men who had put him away.

The journey across the Straits of Gibraltar to the

Spanish mainland was calm, the sea barely a ripple. Harry stood on the deck watching Cueta retreating in the wake of the boat. The sun was out and warmed his head. The hair was growing back and the stubble scratched at his hands. He looked sinister but felt happy.

When he left P. P. Rosales the Consul had driven him to the docks and handed him a ferry ticket to Algeciras and a train ticket to London via Madrid, San Sebastian and Paris. That was it. Harry's look appealed for cash to help him on his way.

"I am sorry," said the Consul "I have already done more than is wise."

Then he relented slipped his hand into his pocket and handed Harry a few notes.

Harry looked at the money 500 pesetas around two British pounds. It was going to be a tough trip.

The train to Madrid had been slow. Stopping at every small town on the way. Harry was hungry and thirsty. He had been on the train for hours, eaten nothing and only drinking water from the non-potable taps. He tried to sleep in the Madrid station but was disturbed by a police patrol who checked and re-checked his passport each time they passed. They were drawn to his shorn head and unkempt clothing. They kept an eye on him until he boarded the morning train. Thanks to Franco the poor were still poor and everywhere. Many carried their food with them as they travelled home for Christmas.

A family, mother, father and two young children, shared the carriage with Harry. The train was full of people returning to their villages for the festivities. Returning with gifts and stories of good fortune. But everybody knew that life was worse in the cities. The mother, barely out of her teens, opened a large hessian bag and handed two filled baguettes to the children. She was beautiful, her hair was glistening black. Her face shone with anticipation and her eyes sparkled with happiness and pride. Her clothes were simple and clean. The father seemed older, beaten, the future of his family weighing him down, drudgery moulding him. His face was dark and deeply lined, his teeth brown stained and broken. He wore a clean white shirt buttoned to the neck, chunky black jacket and grey shapeless trousers, frayed at the bottoms. On his feet were a pair of polished stout boots. He was badly shaven, a region of his neck sprouting black and white strands of hair, long enough to curl over his shirt collar. It looked almost contrived, as though great care had been taken to cut around this small facial oasis. His fingers were fat and swollen. He pulled at the constrains of the top button. Harry focused on the small boy who struggled with a piece of bread as big as himself. After a few minutes the child offered Harry a bite. Harry laughed and declined. The young mother watched as Harry's eyes followed every mouthful the kids were taking. Cheese and sliced tomato fell out of the loosely clutched baguettes onto the floor. The mother opened a bottle flicking off the plastic top and handed it to her husband who drank, his dry lips never touching the neck as he expertly tipped the wine slowly into his throat. She leaned over and offered Harry a thick slice of hard cheese and a chunk of chorizo wrapped in bread. He smiled and received it graciously. The sausage was fiery hot and his eyes watered and his throat dried. The husband laughed and handed Harry the bottle. Harry gulped down the cheap red wine. It was better than vintage Rosales. He went to hand the bottle back, but the husband declined. His wife brought out another bottle and handed it to her husband who drank in the same fashion as before. Harry realised that the lips should never touch the bottle. It was too late, he had the rest of the wine to himself.

The winds swept snow down from the Pyrenees. Harry sat on the platform of San Sebastian railway station. It was Christmas Eve and few trains were running. The temperature hovered around zero. His reefer jacket and clothes engrained with dirt offered little insulation from the cold. It had taken over thirty hours since leaving Algeceris to reach San Sebastian. Lack of food and drink left little energy to fight the numbing cold. The station was all but deserted as he waited on the freezing platforms for the seven a.m. to Paris. The station bar was open he hoisted his bag onto his back and entered the dingy café. Two men, the only customers, sat at separate tables. One looked a forlorn lonely drinker. The other, a stranded traveller, bored and tired. The barman looked up, acknowledged Harry, then continued busying himself with small hour chores. Harry was grateful. The warmth of the bar made him drowsy and he leaned back on the chair. One of the men, the stranded traveller, was eating an omelette and fried potatoes. Harry could smell the goodness as the aroma wafting towards him. He started thinking of his favourite food and decided that what he wanted more than anything was a runny fried egg on a hillock of mashed potatoes with a slice of bread thick with butter and a steaming mug of hot, strong, sweet tea. His face burned as the blood began to circulate again and his eyes closed. When he awoke, minutes, hours maybe only seconds later, the travelling man had gone. The drinker was still deep in his own mind and the barman was nowhere to be seen. The plate of food was shoved into the middle of the table, barely touched. A half empty glass of wine abandoned. Harry sat for a moment and contemplated the remains of the omelette and the fried potatoes.

He picked up his bag and moved to the vacated table. He lunged at the food, forsaking the knife and fork for the swiftness of his hand. He swallowed the omelette in a state of panic and drained the glass of wine, then turned to leave. The travelling man stood blocking his way a puzzled look on his face. He looked down at his plate, ransacked and empty. Then looked into Harry's shifting eyes. Behind the man two Guardia Civil entered on their rounds. Harry's face registered resignation. So close to France so close to freedom.

The Consul had warned Harry to attract as little attention as possible. He had been stopped twice in Madrid. There the station had been busy and the police too harassed with the Christmas rush to bother. The man sat at the table and gestured Harry to sit also. He shouted an order for the barman who finally appeared eyes blinking, running his fingers through his hair, shaking himself awake. He cleaned his hand on a stained cloth and picked up four glasses, shining them on his apron. He filled the glasses with cheap brandy and scuttled to the table. The police scrutinised Harry's passport looking at the picture of a bearded long-haired man, then at Harry's head, then back at the passport. "Merry Christmas," the man said to Harry as he handed him a glass of brandy. The policemen returned his passport and each took the offered glass.

The forlorn drunk staggered to his feet and stumbled towards the door. The Guardia drained their drinks turned and followed the easier target. Harry looked up at the bar clock. It was five past midnight, Christmas Day. There was a Santa Claus.

The cross-channel ferry headed back to the dull skies of Britain. Harry leaned over the rail of the ship and watched as the gulls dipped and dived, circled and screamed in the wake of the boat. There was a theory among ferry crews, that the seagulls had a demarcation line exactly halfway between England and France. In mid channel the gulls from England take over from the French gulls and escort the English bound ship homeward.

The Christmas wine was less vinegary than normal and free. A huge dish of paella was set on the trestle table and served with chunks of warmed bread and olive oil. Never had I looked forward to a meal as much as this. We watched the steaming food cooling as the local dignitaries arrived to inspect and check on our welfare. We waited for the ladies in hats and fine coats to speak a word, say a prayer and leave. The guards watched and flashed a signal to all the prisoners, "Smile and say you love it here." By the time the do gooders had done good and gone the paella was cold. I spooned in the rice and chicken and mussels and prawns and every other bit of nutrition and drained the near vinegar wine. My two prison possessions an aluminium plate and spoon shone like silver candlesticks so thoroughly had they been licked clean.

There had been trouble in the Spanish North Africa territories. The Sahara was under threat from the Moroccan activists. Demonstrations and publicity had brought this problem to the attention of the world. It was something to do with phosphates, not people. The Spanish Legion was put in to quell any disturbances. Three of them were in Rosales. They had deserted and were caught crossing into Ceuta with hashish concealed in fake relief paintings. Super fit rock music fans, tough as bullets, with nothing left to lose. They had not been in Rosales long and were awaiting the fearsome justice of a military trial. Jose was the leader, he was small, the same size wide as he was tall. He was in his early twenties and came from Barcelona.

Louis was only nineteen. A tall, tough youth, who always wore a long black leather coat and Spanish boots. He came from Salamanca outside of Madrid. Wherever he was going after Rosales, he knew it would be for a while. This was his third drug related offence. He was not long out of an army jail. The military didn't like him or his drugs. He told me that he had boiled up and drank a brew made from deadly nightshade, the belladonna plant associated with witches and visions. It held him in a terrifying, insane dream like state for three days he said.

"How often did you take that?" I enquired.

"Just the once." he replied, with a rare smile.

Charlie was a little older than the other legionnaires and had held rank in the force. He had a young family in Madrid. He was very quiet. He read books, played the flute and guitar and seemed gentle. However, he was not gentle. I gravitated towards the legionnaires after Jose had approached me and asked about various words and expressions contained in the lyrics of Bob Dylan's songs. Being a fan I knew most of Dylan's albums and did my best to explain what they meant to me. The evenings in the Brigada were spent smoking and singing the latest hits to the accompaniment of Charlie's guitar.

The locals villians like Carlos and Casablanca, shunned the drug fraternity keeping to themselves at the better end of the Brigada. They thought themselves proper criminals. Wife beaters, rapists, and car thieves, being higher up the socially acceptable ratings than us. There were a couple of members of an organised gang that stole mopeds and smuggled them into Morocco It had taken the customs a while to realise that they were not smuggling cigarettes and whisky but the mopeds themselves. Somewhere at the bottom of the criminal hierarchy but still above the dopers was a bankrupt builder. He cried most of the time. Shame and fear had brought on a nervous breakdown and he either lay weeping on his bunk or sat in silence in the yard.

The Cuetans had the best jobs, working in the warmth of the kitchen or controlling the shower block or the barbers. Thursday was shower and shave day. Cold showers cost nothing, hot showers a small prison fortune. Being shaved the barber, using a new blade was expensive, shaving yourself under supervision with an old discarded blade but no razor, cost only a few pesetas. The barber was a dapper happy sort of person who came from Cueta and was more friendly towards us foreigners. He was also in for smuggling hash into the Spanish enclave. His smuggling technique was simple. He would take the bus to Tetuan, buy some hash, pop it into a parcel and mail it home to himself. All went well for a few months. Then it didn't. He received regular visits from his wife and children. He always had clean clothes and food parcels Juan was determined whilst incarcerated to use his time to secure his future. He looked to Dadi for some insiders advise on how to progress up the trafficking ladder. Dadi's answer was the same for all of us small timers. Go home to your wife and children and get a job as a waiter or barman and enjoy the privileged life you have been given.

Miki, a Yugoslavian, was caught carrying a chair through customs. The Moroccans had many tried and tested methods of smuggling. Filling the legs of a poorly made chair with hash was one of the worst. There would be only one reason a backpacker was carrying a chair out of Morocco and it wasn't to sit on when tired. Whilst the likes of Miki took up the interest of the customs officials another hash laden truck would roll across the border unchallenged and heading for the docks. The quality of Miki's hash was suspect. He discovered that he was not only short changed but short weighted, his kilo of zero zero top notch dope turned out to be 500 grams of henna. He was charged with intent to smuggle contraband and fine the equivalent of ninety British pounds. He had spent two months in Rosales paying the fine off at 225 peseta a day. He still had a month to go. He had appealed to his father, who was once a general in Tito's army, to buy him out. His father had written back saying that he himself had been held in a prison for some three years by anti-fascist rebels and felt that Miki would benefit from the experience.

Hans the Dutchman was going nowhere except insane. He was allowed no contact with the outside world. His father-in-law must have placed some money in high places.

The Capo was the spokesman for the Brigada. He was elected by the prisoners. His job was to keep control. He was an older man, a Spaniard, small, dark and thumbless. Somebody had cut them off many years before. He had been in P. P. Rosales for over thirty years. When the Civil War ended in 1939 he was an officer's batman. He was only 18 years old and married to a beautiful girl. The officer he aided, raped his young bride. He shot the man dead. The normal sentence for murdering an officer was a firing squad. He was shown leniency and given life imprisonment. Every night between ten o'clock and six in the morning four prisoners were selected from a rota, which did not include Carlos, Casablanca or the Capo, to patrol up and down the Brigada. Each doing a two hour watch. This was called Machanalia. The idea being to stop theft, homosexual or any kind of midnight rambling. The favoured shift was the ten until twelve, the least popular the two 'til four. The guard on night duty would invariably catch the prisoner on the two 'til four shift, sitting, dozing or asleep. This resulted in a prison fine and another stint the next night. The wealthier were prepared to pay not to do the two 'til four. I decided that this was going to be my job and began a nightly two 'til four shift. Although I had money at the door, I would need all of it to get back to Britain. I volunteered each night and used the extra prison tokens to supplement my diet.

Without being forewarned, The Capo was to be released. He was excited and scared. He would be going out to nothing. No family or friends, no job and no status. He had respect from the other prisoners for surviving years in a place where few could survive. He had gained credence and credibility in an environment of fear. He was almost gentle despite the deprivation. He had kept control over a Brigada peopled by desperate men, using negotiating skills that would be an asset to a top businessman. No training for freedom here, thirty-five years penal servitude? Be gone in the. morning.

With his departure the Brigada would have to elect another Capo. Carlos who thought he ran the jail anyway, backed by the crazy Casablanca, voiced a strong desire for the job. The legionnaires, Jose, Louis and Charlie, had other ideas. The old Capo warned me not to get involved in the dispute for the Brigada's new leader. "You have too much to lose. You will be out as soon as your money arrives from England." The Capo explained to me the simple system for election. It was more a show of strength than a democratic vote. Candidates backed by their supporters faced each other in the Brigada. A stand-off. All those who didn't want to be included, who didn't want to participate in the vote could lie on their bunks and pull a blanket over their heads. The signal of abstention.

On the evening before the Capo's release, the warden came up to the Brigada switched off the lights and left. In the cell block, Carlos unilaterally declared himself the new Capo. He paraded through the Brigada looking for any opposition, his back-up Casablanca, sneering beside him. Some of the Spanish prisoners started singing mournful laments. In the next Brigada the Moroccans competed, a cacophony of shrill voices set to drown out any disturbances that were about to follow. Louis put on his big leather coat and stamped his feet firmly into his supple Spanish boots. Charlie carefully dismantled his flute, stowing it neatly into his army kit bag. They took their time and when they were ready joined Jose and all three walked up face to face with Carlos. They were outnumbered by Carlos and his fellow Ceutans, who threatened behind him. The old Capo lay on his bunk and pulled his blanket over his face. I looked across at the scene and with trembling hands, followed the Capos lead. Jose head butted Carlos and simultaneously Louis and Charlie jumped on Casablanca. The attack was quick, efficient and soon over. Carlos gave up the moment Casablanca was felled by Charlie. Louis, young and aggrieved, followed through, putting his Spanish boots to good use, crushing them into Casablanca's ribs as Charlie stomped Casablanca's face. Carlos appealed for them to stop. Casablanca had had enough, but the legionnaires had not. They pounded Casablanca into deep unconsciousness. Election over, Jose, Louis and Charlie looked around the Brigada at the few prisoners who were still standing. Jose asked if anybody else wanted to be considered for the job. Nobody spoke. Jose was the new Capo.

Regime changes can be that sudden. The trio of legionnaires took over the running of the jail. Within a couple of days Carlos without the protection of Casablanca, acknowledged Jose's leadership and fell in with the new regime. He continued as the soup orderly but stirred the broth more frequently. He comforted himself with the thought that Jose and the other legionnaires would soon be gone to a military prison and he would be able to return the jail to a proper corrupt footing. Casablanca was taken to a mainland hospital. I never saw him again. Showers, shaves and haircuts became free. A laundry room that contained the washing machine of prison legend was discovered. Gas bottles, made available by the prison authorities at no charge ensured our showers stayed hot. All these concessions had Carlos shaking his head in disbelief unable to understand the new world. A cleaning rota that included everybody was prepared and implemented. The legionnaires inspected the prison and the Brigada to ensure standards improved. The toilet holes were hosed down several times a day and would have been clean enough even for Harry.

Louis, who was only nineteen and destined for a long haul through the Spanish penal system wanted to start a school and take advantage of each other's talents. We were allocated the chapel area of the prison. Charlie started a music class. He acquired a tape machine from Dadi. Once they heard Jimi Hendrix pulsating out of the chapel area, the Moroccans wanted to take advantage of the new education classes and joined in. The wardens were happy about the change in the prisoners' attitude and brought in the latest British and American Rock music tapes.

Playboy had longish hair and always wore dark shaded sunglasses. He was younger than the others guards and looked like he smoked himself, yet he was the hardest to get along with.

In the yard when he was on duty, he banned all ball games. A makeshift ball of old rags and paper would be kicked and thrown around the yard in an attempt at having some sort of fun. Playboy reasoned that we prisoners could kick the ball over the double walls of the jail and someone on the other side could stuff the rags with hashish and kick it back again. He said that would never happen on his shift. It didn't; but within a week it was happening on everybody else's thanks to Juan the Cuetan barber and his family of future soccer stars.

I began teaching English to the prisoners using the words and the meanings of all the latest rock albums. I could speak almost no Spanish except "I am cold. What time is it? and what's the matter man." It was bizarre how Jimi Hendrix singing 'Purple Haze' and 'The Darkside Of the Moon' by Pink Floyd and any one of Dylan's nasal poems mean so much to the Spanish and Moroccans. But I had found a place, a position in the hierarchy. The Brigada settled into the new system. A mini revolution had taken place right in front of my eyes. I hadn't participated or even stood up to be counted. I had too much to lose. So much for being a revolutionary bum. Big Ray was right; it's easy to be a socialists when you're poor and have nothing. Not quite so easy standing up for a cause when failure means you lose the lot.

Little things had become important, things people take as their right, a fresh smell, a glimpse of the world outside. When these unnoticed freedoms are removed dreams take over. And how I dreamed in Rosales. I Paced the cobbled yard with a coat or a blanket over my; head marching up to the wall, turning and marching back again. My mind searched back through my life, trying to make some sense out of it. I realised this was the beginning of withdrawing into my own world. Depression, nature's way of blotting out the harshness.

At night in the Brigada when all had settled. I would try to invoke a happy dream and shut out the wheezing and the snoring, the coughing and sounds that invaded the silence. I had to focus hard to keep a good dream going. Always the pleasant fantasy would give way to the horror of being trapped, escaping and running headlong into my pursuers.

Shona had reached that pre-school stage when every question needed a real answer.

She was getting too smart to be fobbed off with fairy stories. She pestered Harry asking again and again. "Where have you been? What's happened to your hair. Why haven't you got a beard anymore?" Harry slipped back under the covers. Julies' flat opened onto a balcony. She loved plants and in the summer they had sat out in the sun amid pots and tubs that spilled geraniums over the ornate ironwork balcony. The lazy sounds of the streets and the music drifting from the sitting room gave Alley Gardens the feel of New Orleans. In the middle of January, the bitter winds blew straight in from Siberia and howled through the street, rattling the doors and banging at the windows. They had hardly spoken the evening before, just watched the television. A couple of people had called around to invite Harry down to the pub. He wanted to stay with Julie and Shona. Things were strained between them. It would take time. "I visited Sandy in prison. "Julie began. "He was looking well, ten years younger. Almost had me believing in him again. He said that you were worse than he was. He doesn't believe in drugs."

"I don't believe in violence but I'm sure he'll force some on me.

" He was never violent to his own."

"Maybe I could claim to be a long lost cousin then," Harry scoffed. There was a bad feeling starting in his stomach. "and the baby?" asked Harry.

"There is no baby anymore Harry. It was my choice. I can't walk from one mess straight into another. I'm going back to Scotland."

"With Sandy?"

"Sandy did ask me but no. That's finished, over. And so is this place. There is nothing for me here. The dream has gone. Once our children start school they become the poor kids from the wrong end of town. Shona deserves better than that. It happens so quickly, one minute, young and carefree. The next pregnant and living in a dump. Most of you men into crime and drink and drugs."

"I'm not a criminal." argued Harry "just a bit of fun that went wrong."

"Just a bit of fun?

Harry lay back in the bed. He never had that many answers but at this moment he couldn't even figure out a decent question. His dreams of returning the conquering hero had been shattered. He had limped back like a wounded soldier. No matter how he turned the pages the story read the same.

"Do you want me to leave ? I'll go back to Ricky's." Harry offered.

"No," said Julie. "Vicky's there most of the time. You concentrate on getting Ricky out."

"I've got to. I can't leave him there. He'll never survive and if he does he I won't be the Ricky we know any more."

Harry had made a note of everybody he knew who might contribute to the 'Get Ricky out of jail fund'. Jack Nunn's name headed the list. Vicky? she thought her boss may cough up a few hundred. Harry decided to keep Ricky's family out of it. Two thousand pounds was a good deal of money to raise in a couple of week to get it down through Spain and across to Cueta in the allotted time was almost impossible. The Spanish banks held on to any money that was passing through their system for as long as was legally allowed. The Consul had mentioned an alternative route through the foreign office and had given him a name to contact when the money was raised.

Harry turned his collar up as he stepped out of the front door of Julies flat. On either side of the Victorian boulevard, French windows opened onto ornate iron work balconies. It was cold, the grey gulls screeched their misery and shate on the few cars that were jacked up in the street. Alley Gardens was no place to leave a decent tyre. A year had passed, so much had happened, yet nothing had changed. The grey tides came and went. The fishermen still fished and smuggled cigarettes and booze. The ferries still criss-crossed the channel carrying cars and passengers to and from the continent. The rain still swept in riding on another gale. He headed to the Marlow for a beer.

Jan was filling the oven with pies. She looked up and smiled at Harry. "Ray," she shouted. "it's Harry he's out, Mary was right." Big Ray came in laughing.

"Good to see you Harry. Where's Ricky?"

Ray began to pull a beer for Harry.

"He's still in jail."

"Oh shit, I've heard people rot in those places."

"It's not that bad, but it's not that good either."

"Anything I can do Harry anything at all?"

"If you've got a couple of grand sitting around doing nothing, you're our man." laughed Harry.

Harry leaned towards Big Ray. "You know it was Ricky who returned your night safe wallet?"

Big Ray looked up as he handed over the pint of beer.

"I'll do my best Harry but Ricky's been drinking off that for about a year now."

"The little bastard, he never shared any of it with me."

"He doesn't. When you don't see Ricky for a day or two you know he's had a good touch."

"Well, he's redeemed himself now."

Harry unfolded the story of Rosales to Big Ray.

We should have a celebration. When Sandy gets

out. 'The Boppers Last Ball'." chuckled Big Ray. "Yes the Boppers Last Ball." he repeated, tickled by his own humour.

"It will be for someone- me I expect."

After Harry left, I started to learn Moroccan French and soon I could speak a simple stripped down version that helped me in Rosales. The waiting was the thing. All the other European prisoners were praying daily for money to arrive from home to pay their small fines. Time couldn't go fast enough for them. I was as usual doing things arse about face. I was trying to slow time down so that the money would arrive before the judge returned from holiday to take up his duties again. Each day passed was a day closer to my demise. I had heard nothing from Harry. I had told him that Jack Nunn was my best bet. Jack ran a clothing company that manufacturer fake jeans and jackets that he sold on at the London markets as cut priced originals. Jack's idea of a good time was to work 14 hours a day, seven days a week. He was an ex-middleweight fighter. His shoulders were wide and his arms and legs were strong and muscled. His shirts were encrusted under the arms like salt lines on the beach. He was a sweaty bastard in his late thirties with dark hair, a good heart and the ability to make real money almost honestly. He was also a homosexual who tried hard to hold his feelings in check and suppress his desires. Every now and then like a ship's cargo in a hurricane his restraints broke loose. He would go on a bender, get completely pissed and end up in the park toilets looking for boys. Despite his once glowing amateur boxing career, to purge his feeling, he would accept the beatings he always received like a monk his penance. This veering off course was rare however and he usually managed to limit his consumption to a couple of pints of beer. Jack Nunn had a soft spot for me. He has been pestering me to shape up, wear some decent clothes and work for him as his right-hand man for a long time. A proper job, tax and insurance and all the things that were against my anti-capitalist beliefs. It was okay to beg, borrow or steal money but to be enslaved for a set time each day was against my casual approach to life. Harry knew that I had a hold over Jack from way back.

Harry walked up to the industrial estate where Jack Nunn had his clothing factory. The receptionist spoke into the intercom system and called for Jack. Her voice was soft and deep. He came into the office from the factory floor. Although it was cold, the perspiration was trickling down his forehead. He led Harry into his office, pushed some samples off a chair and sat down at his desk.

"So what can I do for you then?" Jack began.

"Do you know the story?" Harry asked.

"I heard you got busted in Morocco or somewhere, silly bastard. Where's Ricky?"

"Still in there. He'll get fifteen years, if I can't raise the money and get him out."

"Bribe money. You can't trust them. Those foreign lawyers they'll take you to the cleaners. How much?"

"£2500 cash."

"Have you gone fucking mad?" replied Jack.

"No, that's how much we need."

"I'll give you two hundred. Pay that back promptly and regularly and I'll see about the rest."

"Not enough time. We've only got until the middle of February."

"Says who?"

"That's when the circuit judge comes over from Cadiz. Ricky says you owe him."

"That was a long time ago."

"What did he do?"

"It's what he didn't do. How about fund raising? Appeal to the public? Nearly innocent drug trafficker languishes in African jail. I'll donate a pair of jeans."

"Seriously Jack we don't have much time." said Harry. "We've got to get him out of there."

"Anybody else you can think of?" asked Jack.

"Not anybody with money."

"Maybe you should just rob a bank."

"What in conjunction with the local bus service? Armed robber flees on the number twenty seven." Jack slumped down deeper into the chair. His brow furrowed and he looked into Harry's eyes. "You know something Harry? There are many ways to make real money out there." he gestured with a flaying arm. "but you've got to pay your dues. You've got to pay some tax and insurance, get on the books, get into the system. Keep them off your back. I'm thinking of expanding. I'm sick of making fake American originals. I can see the day when everybody's going to be clad in denim from the dosser in the doorway to highfliers in the city. The aspiring middle classes are losing their roots. But come the weekend they still want to pretend that they are solid working folks and they wear jeans to prove it. I want my own brand name. My own distribution network and my own big mansion in the country. Sod all this let's be poor together stuff. Sod all this agonising protest shit. All your millionaire rock stars and folk singers they're not wandering down that long and lonesome highway. They're luxuriating in fancy hotels in the Hollywood hills." He stopped as his face reddened, and the veins started to thicken on his neck. "Blood pressure." he explained as the sweat started to trickle down his brow. "Ricky helped me out once, a while ago. I'll never forget that. I could have gone away for a long time. I am going to need someone like Ricky, Someone I can trust. My business is the same as yours, regardless of the product. Buy something for four pence and sell it for sixpence, happy days. Buy something for sixpence and sell it for four pence you will become unhappy. It's that simple. There is no need to go tearing up the Moroccan mountainside. There is plenty here to be exploited. There's a whole fashion-conscious generation out there, waiting. And they're all into a little danger, a little edginess, a little rock and roll. If you guys put the same time, energy and commitment into a legitimate business, you would be a hell of a lot better off than you are now. Think about it. Julie and Vicky won't be hanging around with a couple of losers for long. Believe me when the villains in the city twig the amount of money that can be made from drugs they won't come calling with a friendly joint. You guys won't stand a chance. I'll put up what I can, but when he gets out, Ricky has to work for me all legal and proper until he's repaid me. Get what you can from who you can and I'll see what I can dig up."

The sun came out and brightened up the day. Colour reappeared and the grey sea sparkled. His step quickened and he felt better. He called back at Julie's flat and collected his clothes to take to the Laundromat, everything smelled of Rosales. The windows of the laundry were steamed up on the inside. The rivulets of condensation racing down the glass to collect in a puddle on the floor. There was a bank of industrial washing machines and tumble driers the clothes whirring and slapping the metal cylinders, zips clanking out a slow rhythm. An old man was sitting on a chair reading a book. He was wearing a thick insulated fireman's coat, padded against heat but just as effective against the cold. The old man watched Harry as he tipped the bag of washing into the open top loader. A pair of Julies black pants with a red heart motif fell to the floor. The old man moved swiftly to retrieve them. When Harry turned, the old man was sitting back in the chair, the knickers just peeking out of his jacket pocket. The old man's face glowed in anticipation. Harry had no intention of spoiling his afternoon treat. Harry left the laundrette and walked the few yards to the Working Men's club. Not many workers had visited since it had been taken over by the Peoples Republic of Jimmy Dawes. The front security door was lying open. A van was badly parked taking up half the pavement. Harry squeezed past the vehicle and climbed the stairs, the carpet sticking to his feet like hot tar on a summer's day. The light from the outside world beamed up like an old fashioned cinema projector. Two men were struggling with a

Chicago style one armed bandit. The Machine man's empire was expanding. During the week he allowed the fruit machines to pay out a reasonable percentage, but come the weekend he adjusted the settings to guarantee the odds in favour of the Machine man. Why the gamblers thought that they could win, always surprised him. The odds were stacked against success.

"Well, well," said the Machine man "hail the conquering hero comes. What went wrong this time?

"Fuck off."

"Oh dear, that's no way to speak to a friend who might have a job for you."

"What have you got?"

"Nothing. You're yesterday's bad news;" he paused. "Oh wait a minute," he spoke as if concerned. "I may be able to give you a driving job. It will only be temporary. You can pick Sandy up from the nick for me if you like? I'll give you something for petrol and enough for a first aid kit. You've a couple of weeks to think about it," he laughed. The Machine man gloated as he told Harry about his regular visits to the prison to keep Sandy updated on the situation with Julie. "Sandy is chewing on the furniture in his cell, raging with a year of fermenting grudges. It looks like you are going to get a beating for something you have already lost," the Machine man said knowingly. Jimmy Dawes came out of the back office and greeted Harry. "Where's the suntan Harry? I heard you were over wintering in Africa.

A few men lounged at the bar which was strewn with dirty glasses and full ashtrays from the night before. There was a large sign handwritten in a Jimmy's faltering style. 'This club's management accepts no responsibility for stolen property or possessions and that includes drink and drugs.' After a beer Harry returned to the launderette and transferred the damp clothes into the tumble drier. The old man had gone. He went back to the bar to wait the thirty minutes it took for the drying cycle to complete. Jimmy came over with a couple of cans of export lager and sat beside Harry at the table. The Machine man was busy shouting at his new staff. They would be unpaid, at his beck and call, have to put up with his verbal abuse and thank him profusely for wasting their time. Only folks like Sandy MacLean and Paddy Murphy could handle the Machine man's megalomania. He was frightened of them. So was everybody else. "What's with the cans of beer?" asked Harry "run out of draught?"

Jimmy laughed. "Run out of brewers daft enough to deliver. Funny lot the brewers they get all humpy when you don't pay. They take it personal."

"Strange that." said Harry. " when everybody

knows you don't care who you rip off."

"Never ripped you off though Harry. Well apart from Mary. How did you get on with my tent?" He stopped speaking to gulp at his tin of beer. "God that tent holds a few memories for me and Mary."

"Yes we noticed them," said Harry. "you forgot to include the tent poles."

"Oh we never bothered with stuff like that. We just got under it and got on with it. Course we never went far afield. We didn't want to arouse suspicion."

"Whose suspicion?" asked Harry.

Jimmy looked Harry straight in the eye. "Yours mainly. You were living with Mary at the time." Harry watched Jimmy lose interest as he began to explain the complexity of getting Ricky out of Rosales. Jimmy became restless his eyes flicked and darted around the dingy bar area. Jimmy quickly interrupted. "Just leave him there. It's the way it goes. You got out, he didn't. The luck of the draw. We've got a good thing coming off in Holland. Something anybody can make in their bathroom with a few easy to find chemicals. Only trouble is one of the ingredients is a bit hard to source legally. We've had a bit of a problem getting hold of it. The last guy to try, broke into the pharmaceutical suppliers but instead of getting the goods and leaving, he started sampling other products. Next morning they found him dead. That's created a vacancy, the jobs yours if you want it?"

Liam Knox, Mary's youngest brother, struggled through the door of the club carrying a large laundry bag. He began taking out various items of clothing and auctioning them off to the lunchtime drinkers. He held up a pair of faded denim jeans. Harry looked at them with interest. They might just fit him. It only took him a few seconds of scrutiny to realise that they were his own jeans. The Knoxes had been passing variations of the laundromat scam down the family line for some time. "They're my fucking denims you little bastard." shouted Harry. Liam's face broke into a wide grin. "Oh hi Harry" he says "how are you doing? I heard you were away. Sorry mate didn't know they were your jeans?" Harry was rising from the table. Liam Knox was still a youth but already he had the look and the confidence of a man with back up. He was tall with a mop of natural blonde curling hair. Despite his young age he was already showing signs of conflict. A couple of untreated wounds had formed scars on his cheeks and his nose had the charm of an unfixed break. Just as long as his youth held, these would be the visible blemishes of an active member of the warrior class. Harry realised that young Liam was no longer a kid. He would have to negotiate. "What else have you got of mine there?"

"Nothing else worth having. There was an old boy already at it when I went in. I rescued your jeans mate."

"Well done Liam very noble of you. Can I have them back?"

"You can buy them back. If it wasn't for me liberating them they would have been long gone."

"Ah." smiled Harry "That old harbour philosophy"

"You were lucky it was me what robbed you. Fucking amazing."

"Okay how much are they worth, a beer, two beers?"

"Got any hash? It's like a fucking desert here."

"Can I have my jeans back please Liam," said Harry with weariness. "we were caught and imprisoned. Ricky is still in there."

"Go on then I'll settle for a beer," said Liam with resignation. "but don't tell anybody. People might think I've gone soft."

Harry stepped onto the high street not sure which way to go. He walked down to the harbour. The grey sun glistened on the incoming tide. The sea breeze was cold and the boats that had been beached by the low tide began to shift and move with the incoming sea. The fishing was like the rest of the town, it had seen better days. The few boats left in operation in the harbour were not as brightly painted as the postcards sold in the souvenir shops depicted. The red rust oozed along the rivets as the metal reverted to its iron-ore origins. The wooden hulled boats were in need of serious work. The riggings sang in the wind and accompanied the rhythmic slapping of the sea. The small row boats were the first to bob back to life as the tide maintained its onslaught into the harbour. Hulls ground into the concrete wall rattling at their chain moorings. It was easy to see where those depressing sea shanties came from.

Most of the sea food stalls were closed for the winter. Things would pick up again come Easter, but that was still a while away. Only one stand opened every morning, 'Bills' seafood stall. Cockles, Whelks, prawns from Norway, jellied eels in fancy glasses, bottles of chilli vinegar, salt and pepper to taste. Bill was Ronnie Page's uncle he was maybe sixty, thinning hair combed back, his red cheeks sprouted a couple of days stubble, his eyes were fast moving and his mind alert. A big man who seemed even bigger wrapped in layers of thick wool jumpers. He had not worked at anything apart from the stall since the family boat was auctioned off for a quarter of its value in a bankruptcy sale. This was his contact with the world. It was also the meeting place of every villain or aspiring villain in the town. Over a plate of jellied eels, men with no known incomes, caught up on the news, the who's screwing who? Then the lunchtime session in the pubs meeting fellow loafers all working out ways to get enough money to continue the idyllic life of doing as little as possible, for the greatest reward, until the good times returned. Surely the true goal of mankind. Certainly the only goal of the winter unemployed down the harbour.

Harry wasn't too keen on things that could be seen to have once been alive. He preferred his fish in battered fingers from the frozen food section of the bigger stores. When Harry arrived the rain slanted in and Bill began packing up the stand. He threw scraps over the sea wall and watched the ugly gulls as big as eagles diving to retrieve them. "We've got a pact," he laughed as Harry stopped to watch the squawking commotion, "I feed them every day and they shit on my competitors stall instead of mine."

"Does it work?" shouted Harry above the screeching. "looks like they shit on whatever they want, just like every other harbour dweller." Bill carried on with his work.

"Anybody about?" asked Harry.

"No." said Bill. "nothing doing. Heard you were in a bit of trouble, you and Ricky.

"Ricky's still in it, up to his neck in it."

Harry helped Bill pack up the stall and wheel it towards his lock up.

You knew my nephew Ronnie well didn't you?"

"He was more a friend of Ricky's, but I did like him?" replied Harry.

"Everybody liked Ronnie, well nearly everybody. He never meant any harm. Just seemed to think the world was for free. He was my sister's only child, she spoiled him, gave him everything. When he was a boy, he helped me all the time. He knew everybody and everybody knew him, he was safe down here. He should have just stuck to what we do best. Smuggling fags and booze, good honest work, appreciated by everybody. Then all this nonsense about revolution and drugs. He never understood any of that. He was a victim."

Harry liked Ronnie but never thought of him as a victim, he was a good enough guy as long as you didn't leave your girlfriend or your unemployment Giro in his path. He'd cash one and screw the other just as soon as your back was turned. Families must see something different in their own folks, an ability to blur and smooth away the faulty edges.

"Yes he was a good lad. A couple of years in the Arctic fishing for cod would have sorted you lot out. You came home, didn't even know the wife anymore. That was the life."

"People don't just travel for work Bill. For some it's holidays, romance, adventure."

"Oh we had our romance and adventure. I married two Inuit girls once, both on the same trip. They would do anything to marry a British sailor you didn't just get to shag em, they paid you as well. They would get a pension for life if you didn't come back."

Harry didn't want to get Bill started. But Bill started anyway.

"When I was Ronnie's age all I needed was a good set of oilskins, a hot meal and a couple of pints of beer. Fucking brilliant. I had the pick of all the birds around here. Didn't need drugs then. There were a few dishonest villains about but we always felt safe."

"Yes." thought Harry. "the harbour dwellers always felt safe but the same couldn't be said for some unsuspecting fool wandering into their territory with a pocket full of cash" Bill stopped outside his lock up. It was hewn out of the cliff side at the back of the fishermen's cottages, guarded by heavy metal doors built to stop intruders and second world war bombs. The doors were painted black.. Bill looked around as he dragged the metal against the scraped cobbled stonework. Inside, the cave was bigger than the average house "Same temperature winter or summer," Bill said.

He switched on the lights "Did you know what Ronnie was up to?" Bill asked.

"Haven't seen him since last summer." Harry replied truthfully. Bill walked into the back of the storage shed. He pulled back a dust sheet. Underneath was an old Jaguar car the sort that small-time crooks always bought. One day they would have nothing the next they would be cruising around in a movie set jaguar. If the top went down all the better. They were always wondering who had grassed them up when they were dragged into to answer questions about the latest robbery. Bill unlocked the door of the vehicle. Bits of engine parts and tools were strewn in the interior of the once plush motor. A blue box was lying amid the debris of rags and spark plugs. Bill lifted out the box and opened it. There, wrapped in cellophane and stamped with a gold imprint were five bars of what looked like top-quality hashish. "You'll know what this is?" asked Bill quietly. "I found it a few weeks back when I was looking for a screwdriver. There was a few quid in a bag as well. But I knew what that was." He smiled.

"I've a fair idea." said Harry.

"At first I thought it was plastic explosives. I was going to call the police. All that revolutionary nonsense, but I figured it might be valuable."

"Give me an hour or two. Have you told anybody about this yet?" Harry asked.

"Not a chance, people around here can't be trusted." he paused, "I should know, we're all related. A bigger bunch of grabbing bastards you will not find."

"I was going to approach Jimmie Dawes but he seems to be going mad at the moment. I don't like him much anyway. I've always blame him for leading Ronnie astray. His father was the same. Always wanted to be top dog."

"Every generation has its casualties Bill." Said Harry, "Nature's way of keeping us down I suppose."

Harry's mind was already racing ahead of the game. The Lord himself had intervened and contributed to the 'Get Ricky Out Fund', and no mistake.

It had been quite a weekend for Vicky. She stepped off the train at the station and walked down through the underpass her heels clicking like a child's stick rattling on a railing. She headed straight to Julies' place. As she turned the corner into Alley Gardens the sun broke through and she felt safe. People who didn't know the gardens, had it down as a druggies paradise, an open all hours bordello and a place to go if you wanted to get stabbed to death. All three were true at various times but the population changed as frequently as the tides. It was an area of cheap flats, students and drifters and a growing core of young single mothers trying to cope. The colourful mix was provided by an art school that dominated the thinking of the area. The pubs and bars were aglow with the fresh ideas of youth and the bright clothes and scanty designs of the intellectually and sexually aware. Things were going to change for the modern girls. No longer for them the brutality of too many children, too little money and drunken men. That was the theory anyway the truth was always different. What scared Vicky was, how long before she became pregnant like so many of the other girls in Alley Gardens. How long before her dreams were put on hold and she was bathing a baby in the kitchen sink, wet clothes strung on a line above the cooker, everything smelling of stale food. How many nights sitting home alone waiting for Ricky to return from the bar or from pursuing some hopeless deal? I've invested in him, she thought, filled him full of petrol and oil but I just can't seem to steer him in the right direction. And now this.

Julie answered the door. The sparkle had gone out of her eyes. She was thinner than she should have been, life was beginning to beat her down. The two women had become firm friends over the year and Julie was always pleased when

Vicky came around. Vicky could keep her laughing until her stomach ached with tales of the music business. The excesses of the rock bands and their foolishness and pretensions. She had the low down on them all. So many of them playing the working class kid made bad, when most of them were from middle class privileged backgrounds. The shrewder managers and wild child rock stars would rather talk about off-shore investment funds and percentages than anything associated with music. Working in the studio had opened her eyes to the amount of money that was sloshing about. "Where's Shona?" she asked.

"Pre-school today. She starts the infants after Easter."

"Wow where's the time gone?"

"So any luck getting a loan from the boss?" enquired Julie.

Vicky reached into her bag and pulled out a wedge of notes.

"Five hundred pounds. It's a start."

"Brilliant how did you get that?" asked Julie.

"I fucked the boss." replied Vicky.

"And he gave you five hundred quid?"

"He loaned me five hundred pounds, I have to pay it back out of my wages. Screwing him was just to secure the loan, an arrangement fee."

"What was it like?"

"I've had worse times, just can't remember when." Vicky's eyes filled up. "He must have been fit once. I'm sure he's read all the manuals, all the magazines but by the time he got around to getting it on I was bored with the whole performance and half asleep. I felt like a prostitute. I suppose I am a prostitute. Ricky better be worth it,"

"You're not a prostitute Vicky. It's just a one off that's all, forget it.

Julie and Vicky settled down with a cup of coffee.

"I told Harry this morning that I'm leaving. Things have got to change. Harry is a great guy. Just aimless and stupid. If he stays around much longer, he will end up in a prison that he can't get out of."

"Do you love him?" asked Vicky

"I think so yes. It's been strained. If we could make a clean break. A fresh start. Shona starting off her life like this. It's all wrong. The dream is over for me. Harry says he will stop all this nonsense and get a proper job. I wish I could believe him."

"Does Harry want to leave here?"

"First he's got to get the money together to for Ricky. Your five hundred is a great start."

Harry climbed the stairs to Julie's flat he felt nervous. His stomach was unsettled. He heard Julie speaking so he made enough noise for her to hear as he opened the door. He popped his head around the partitioned kitchen and smiled as he saw Vicky. She held up the five hundred pounds in triumph. Harry gave her a quick hug,

"The boss lent me this." she said "It's a start."

Harry looked at the money."Hope you didn't have to do too much for it?"

Harry turned to Julie beaming.

"I may have found the solution to the problem. Ronnie Page stashed the dope he ripped off the Dutch and a bag of money in his uncle's boat hut. A couple of kilos of good quality hash. His uncle wants it out of there pronto. There was some money too, but Bill's had that away. If that roadie mate of yours and his rich musical friends up at the mansion recording studios are still on the lookout for a bit of dope Vicky, we're all are in money."

"Don't you think that maybe the police will be watching you?" asked Julie.

Harry sat down beside her and smiled. "Maybe," he said, getting excited, "but we have to get this sorted before things go wrong."

"Do you not think things have gone wrong already?" asked Julie.

"We're still in with a chance." Harry reasoned. "Vicky's five hundred, at least five hundred from Jack Nunn. Good old Ronnie Page he did not die in vain."

"You know something," said Julie "if you channeled your talents and energy into something legal you couldn't help but succeed."

"Funny that's just what Jack Nunn said."

At eleven o'clock on a Wednesday morning the Marlow bar would normally be as quiet and reflective as a crematorium waiting room. Hangovers dominated. The first drink, the finest cure was always swallowed in silence. A nod and a grunt of recognition were all the drinkers' protocol required. The shaky and the sad stood like apparitions at the bar or sat in a corner camouflaged by their stillness. Today was different. They had been drinking since the doors opened at ten and already the atmosphere was far too charged for the locals. The jukebox pounded out the latest hits and a group of men dressed in denims, high-heeled boots, dazzling shirts and fancy jackets were making more noise than Big Ray was happy with. They were drinking American whiskey and filling the till faster than a crowded bar on a weekend. They traipsed backwards and forwards to the toilet rubbing their noses on return and becoming louder and louder. Nothing could mask the sweet pungent odour of exotic smoke. A quiet man dressed in purple trousers wearing a pair of boots painted in the colours of the American flag sat more subdued than the others He wasn't white and he wasn't black, more like a high cheeked American Indian, his hair teased up like a halo curled around the brim of a black fedora hat.

Harry opened the door of the bar, the goods secure in a shopping bag. He had chosen a Wednesday because the pub was always quiet first thing. He didn't expect this racket. A large man with a barrel chest came stumbling over to greet Harry. He was drunk and the crumpled white suit he was wearing was stained with beer and bits of food, a black tee shirt struggled to contain a belly that hung over a thick leather belt. "I brought the band. Come and meet them they are going to be BIG BIG BIG." he emphasised in a slurred Irish accent.

"I thought rock bands didn't get up in the morning?" said Harry.

"They don't. They've been recording all night."

"For fucks sake," said Harry "this was meant to be cool. Just you and me and the money."

"Ah just a bit of cover." He laughed his eyes sparkling like frost in the sunlight. Harry looked over at Big Ray. Big Ray was far from happy.

"Heh landlord a pint of your finest for my friend

here," shouted the Irish man, spilling more beer down his white suit. He rubbed at it with an uncoordinated hand. "Oh shit looks like I'll have to buy another jacket."

"Let's get this done," said Harry, "I've places to be." Harry stood at the bar and Big Ray looked down at him with beady eyes scrunched up behind a pair of reading glasses. "Get what has to be done, done," he hissed "and get that fucking lot out of here before the bloody police arrive."

In the third week of February the money came through and I was released on bail. I said farewell to the Legionnaires who had become close friends in a short time. I collected my money from the door. I'd been frugal and thanks to the Legionnaires and Dadi there was still enough to make it back to Britain. Dadi, if things didn't change would be in and out of Rosales forever or until it was the turn of someone else to take care of the business. It mattered nothing to him. In his eyes he was political but in the eyes of the law, a common criminal. He was one of a generation of Berbers who were determine, with help, to capitalise on the proximity of the marijuana production to Europe. For him there was no sentiment. All he wanted was to improve the lot of himself and his extended family. Before I left I shook Dadi's hand and he advised me never to attempt smuggling again. "Backpackers and bold amateurs are jail fodder," he explained, "go home, get a wife, find work. You have freedom and opportunity. Why do this?" he laughed, "we have nothing, this is our only chance."

The British Consul met me outside the big gates and drove me to the customs post. The van was almost buried in sand. The grey-haired customs official was standing by the vehicle smiling. He shook my hand greeting me like a friend and wished me luck. I got into the van and turned on the ignition. It started first time.

The grey-haired man leaned through the window. "Anything to declare?"

"Only a lesson hard learned."

The British Consul handed me a ticket for the ferry.

"You have only two days to get out of Spain," he said, "don't stop until you get to France and don't set foot in Spanish territory for at least thirty years." The grey-haired man saluted and waved me on my way. I realised I was just part of their economy.

When the boat docked in Spain the van was the first vehicle off the boat. I handed the customs officer the letter that had been given to me by the British Consul. The customs official handed it back and waved me through. I stopped at a café bar just outside the Spanish harbour. Despite having my rations supplemented by the food in the Moroccans yard I had lost weight in Rosales. Although it was morning the bar was full. I was hungry and ordered a beer and a baguette. The bar man loaded the bread and watched in amazement as I devoured the food. "Ah, P. P. Rosales" he laughed, rubbing his hand over my stubble head. He walked to the side of the bar and made a telephone call. I watched him with suspicion. A few minutes later I almost choked on his snack. In front of the bar, a van marked Douane was discharging half a dozen customs officers. They marched straight into the bar. I downed the beer and stuffed what I could of the squid loaf into my mouth. The barman greeted the Customs officers as they swung onto a row of stools, loosened their jackets and ordered their breakfast.

With 800miles to the French border I stopped only for fuel, a piss and something to eat. Every headlight in the mirror, every policeman's glance and every motorbike cop who cruised alongside before leaning into another problem had my heart racing. In the morning I crossed the unmanned customs post into France. I had made it.

When I drove off the ferry in Dover I was waved through British customs without as much as a where you been? Something was wrong. I had felt sure that I would be stopped, searched and questioned. I parked up the van in Alley Gardens next to two unmarked police vehicles with telltale aerials swaying in the chill February wind. A young customs officer and two hardened members of the newly formed local drug squad were waiting for me. Harry, Julie and Vicky stood in silence. The boyish customs officer spoke. "Stay where you all are. No speaking or touching." I ignored him and shook Harry's hand. "Cheers mate." I said. I embraced Julie, then moved towards Vicky and hugged her like a child hugs his mother. Tears were in my eyes as I looked around my flat. Vicky had transformed it from hostel to a home. Stains on the walls had been replaced with posters. The kitchen area was clean and bright. The young customs man who looked like he was still at school took command. "Check the van," he instructed one of the local police officers. "There may be something there that the Spanish didn't find." I accompanied the local officer who was tall, lean and bored, down the stairs and into the van.

"What were you guys up to?" asked the policeman.

"Just another balls up," I replied.

"The Customs don't think so," he said, giving the

van a once over. He lit up a cigarette. "He's keen, is that one. He has you lot involved in an international drug smuggling ring. The dark girl he sees as the Italian connection."

"The dark girl? Vicky? She was born in London."

"Involved in politics though," said the drug squad detective. "they have her on film. You too."

"What?"

"Last years protest march?"

 "That was a load of crap."

"Problems with the Irish bombers. The government reckons that it's drug money that's funding the show."

"So where do we fit in?" I asked.

"You got caught," he laughed. "you'll do. You fit the profile. Mid-twenties, no ties, political. Just the type they're looking for."

He opened the back of the van and climbed in.

"Here get in," he said. "keep out of the way for five minutes." He drew on his cigarette. "Did you catch any Spanish football games when you were down there?"

"No." I said. "but I saw a few assholes fighting bulls."

The fresh faced customs man took me through

into the bedroom. There was a cheap chest of drawers a bed and a wardrobe. The furniture was secondhand household rejects. The first drawer the customs man opened was filled with Vicky's underwear. He made a show of picking up panties and bras. "Wear this stuff often?" he teased.

"Whenever the mood takes me," I replied.

"Nice little gaff you have here. You guys always seem to get by, no work, no job, no obvious means of income but always a nice gaff. And a girl" When he said 'Gaff', it sounded as if he had been practicing the word in his bathroom mirror. "Couldn't' get much more basic," I said "two rooms and a kitchen."

"More than I've got," he moaned. On top of the cupboard was a blue case. The customs man looked up at it. "Where do you get a case like that?

" I've no idea." I said." I had never seen it before".

 A smile crept over the inexperienced man's face.

"You've never seen it before." He mocked.

He called to the remaining drug squad officer who was chatting up Julie in the front room. The policeman stubbed out his cigarette and entered the bedroom. "Take that case to pieces," he ordered. "He claims never to have seen it before." The Drug squad officer pulled it down and burst it open. It was empty. "Check for false compartments, cut it up if necessary," ordered the youthful sleuth, "Where could you get a case like that? India, Bangkok. Tangiers?"

"Any British high street, it looks perfectly normal to me, It's just not mine."

"Cut it open." smiled the customs officer.

The policeman took out a small penknife and cut into the lining of the case. "Nothing here sir." In the chest of drawers, concealed under a pair of old jeans was a bag of what looked like demerara sugar. The bag had been opened and then folded over and sealed with a clothes peg. "What's this?" smirked the young customs man

"I don't know. It looks like brown sugar to me," I replied. He licked his middle finger, then dipped it into the open bag. He withdrew it and offered it to the policeman to taste. Reluctantly the officer took the offered finger into his mouth and sucked it.

"Well?" asked the customs man, "What do you think that is."

"Demerara sugar sir," said the Drug Squad officer, "There's a sugar shortage sir, my wife's the same, sugar hidden all over the house."

"I think that we are all done here now." said the red-faced youth sweeping his hair back from his eyes. "We'll be back," he threatened

"When?" asked Harry.

"That's for us to know and you to find out," said the Customs officer regaining his composure. The local drug squad officers squirmed and left.

In the bedroom Vicky was going through the chest of drawers, putting her underwear into a blue laundry bag. "What else did he touch?" she asked, "I feel sick. He looked like a little pervert. "

"Pillar of society" I laughed grapping Vicky and pulling her towards me. "I'm the dirty pervert. What I haven't done to you in my dreams."

Harry was taking things badly. He stood in front of the kitchen mirror in Julie's flat, he was stripped to the waist his body pale and thin. Although he was six foot tall he had lost too much weight in Rosales. His hair was growing back on his head but he hardly recognised the man in front of himself. If they had succeeded, things might have been different. He held a knife in a thrusting position. What are you doing?" I asked.

"Taking a lesson from your story of the legionnaires. How to beat your opponent before he knows what's fucking hit him." answered Harry as pulled at a roll of thick masking tape. "Here," he continued "tape this to my back." He held up the knife.

"Do you know how painful that can be?"

"What getting stabbed?"

"No, that tape it'll make your eyes water peeling it off your hairy back.

"I don't have a hairy back," Harry said. Twisting and turning to catch a glimpse in the mirror.

"Ah fuck this," he said throwing the knife into the cluttered sink. "The way my luck's running I'll end up stabbing myself." We walked slowly down to the Marlow. The pub was almost empty. Big Ray and Jan had made up a few sandwiches. There was a banner over the bar welcoming both Sandy MacLean and me back home. The atmosphere was tense, most people feared Sandy yet fawned over him, desperate to deflect any of his anger away from them. Sandy could turn hostile in mid-sentence as if a switch had been thrown. It was scary to watch, it was scarier being on the receiving end of his alcoholic hatred.

"The story is he's down the harbour pissed up and holding court in the Anchor. A pocket full of money and a brain full of mince. I've got an extension, they'll all be up soon enough." explained Big Ray. "

All evening we nursed our beer, sipping rather than gulping. It was strange I wanted to drink until I fell down, but If we were going to get a beating from Sandy and his merry men, we wanted to see it coming. The sandwiches began to curl at the edges and so did the few customers. Big Ray began recanting tales of bygone days when he was something big in the city of London. An overweight window cleaner, but he never gave that bit away. Every time the door opened the bar turned as one.

Jack Nunn was the first to arrive ahead of the party struggling up from the harbour. "Haven't seen you for a while Ricky," he said. "have this one on me. Three pints Ray and something for yourself. "

"Thanks for the money," I said. "I will definitely pay you back."

"That you will Ricky boy that you will." You only got the money on the strength of you starting to work for me. "Didn't Harry explain?".

"I'll dock your wages every week until it's paid." said Jack.

I looked at Harry, he had forgotten to mention this. I'd just been sold to Jack Nunn.

"When do I start?" I asked.

"That's the spirit Ricky," he laughed scooping up his beer. "let's wait until we see if you get through the weekend. You are on Sandy's hit list as well. Friend of an enemy and all that psycho logic. I thought I would get up here before him, to give my new employee a hand. I'm nothing if not a caring boss."

"I know he is coming but I'm not running," said

Harry "Sometimes you have to stand up and be counted."

"Yeah counted out." When he hits you, go down and stay down and hope he doesn't kill you." advised Jack.

Sandy MacLean and his band of hangers-on were nearing the Marlow. Sandy was singing at the top of his voice but what the song was only he knew. Sandy's capacity for alcohol was legendary and although he swayed and stumbled he was still in control. Jimmy Dawes, the Machine man and every harbour renegade were egging him on as they staggered to the Marlow and the showdown. There was a noticeable lack of women in the crowd that entered the bar. Jack Nunn headed for the toilet. "Beers gone straight through me." he claimed. He made it to the cubicle next to the urinals, sat down, snubbed the lock and waited. Harry sweated, Big Ray leaned under the bar and held onto the truncheon that he polished with care every week.

"Hold up." said Big Ray to the entering revelers, "This is a double celebration for Ricky as well as Sandy so we don't want any trouble in here."

 "There won't be," said Sandy walking up to Harry and sticking his face inches from his. Harry smelled Sandy's beer-soaked breath, "Been waiting for this moment Harry my old mate. How are you?"

The time had come, the sweat burst out on Harry's forehead and trickled into his eyes. He had not fled, he had not tried to hide, that would have only postponed the inevitable. He walked towards the toilets not turning his back completely on Sandy. The music from the jukebox pounded out an old Jerry Lee Lewis number. "You shake my nerves and you rattle my brains." Harry turned as he entered the toilet and Sandy closed in on him. He knew the only option was attack but his body seemed frozen he felt sick and his legs started to shake. "Goodness gracious great balls of Fire" the Killer roared from the juke box. Harry lunged forward attempting to butt Sandy on the nose. Drunk as he was Sandy had been a fighter all his life. He saw it coming and dropped his head. A loud crack like the echo of rutting stags could be heard in the bar. The piano stomping Louisiana rocker rocked on. Sandy stepped back and Harry slumped to the floor.

"You bastard." shouted Sandy kicking him in the stomach. "Get up I'm going to kill you."

The cubicle door opened and Jack Nunn emerged. "Fairy fucking Jack. I might have fucking known." Sandy hissed. "peoples champion and lover of little boys. You've put on weight". He dived towards Jack throwing a blow to his ample stomach. Jack swung a punch from his toes that caught Sandy just below the heart. Sandy bent double for a fraction of a second, then replied with a punch to Jack's groin. Jack fell into the urinal pulling Sandy down with him. Sandy grabbed hold of Jack's ear and tore at it until he felt it give. Jack started squealing like a braking train. Big Ray rushed into the toilet to stop the mayhem, truncheon at the ready.

Four minutes later the party began. Sandy boasted to the crowd that he had beaten the pair of them and enough was enough. There was a piss up to be enjoyed. The hangers-on, hung on his every word. They fawned and flattered and welcomed him back, eager for his ferocious eye to pick out anybody but themselves. Sandy's head cocked and turned like a bird of prey. He had dreamed of this day for a year. He was back and it had all been worth it. He was fit again, strong and ready to rule for another few years. Bar room politics was a strange game but not if you made up the rules.

Harry basked in the glory of standing up to Sandy as Julie fussed over the egg size bump that was growing on his forehead. Sandy and Jack were soon swapping old fight stories. The crowds barged in and the music blared out late into that February night. By the time Big Ray called last orders there were few drinkers still able to stand. Jack and Sandy left the bar together, propping each other up. Jack turned to me as he was leaving. "See ya Monday morning seven prompt." He held out his hand as if to shake mine. As I leaned over, he reached down and grabbed me by the balls. "Gotcha." he crowed.

Harry awoke next to Julie. His carrier bag of clothes packed ready for the trip. Harry had never been to Scotland before. In his mind it was peopled by Sandy MacLean types pissed up and dangerous. But Julie assured him that most of the Scottish maniacs were living in the South East of England. Vicky and me went around to say goodbye. The van was loaded, the sun was shining and the cold wind had dropped. We said our farewells, the girls hugging each other in tears. "Take care of him Julie," I said with sadness, "he's even softer than he looks." Harry fired up the old transit van and rolled down the window.

"You know?" said Harry "this could be one of those defining moments in life."

"You know? I said, "this time, you might just be right."

Seaside Stories caricatures an era of excess, irresponsibility and downright dumbness. A must for the modern historian.

Drink, drugs and other delights, a generation's attempts to philosophise failure. Seaside Stories does just that.

photographs Ray Cachart ©

Printed in Poland
by Amazon Fulfillment
Poland Sp. z o.o., Wrocław

53808992R00099